Fred Hoyle, F.R.S., well known as an astronomer, writer,
broadcaster, and television personality, was born at
Bingley, Yorkshire, in 1915 and educated at Bingley
Grammar School and Emmanuel College, Cambridge.
A Fellow of St John's College, Cambridge, he was a
university lecturer in mathematics from 1945 to 1958,
when he was appointed Plumian Professor of Astronomy
and Experimental Philosophy, a post he held until 1973.
He has been Professor of Astronomy at the Royal
Institution of Great Britain since 1969.
Since 1956 he has been a staff member at the Mount
Wilson and Palomar Observatories, where he is able to
use the world's largest reflector telescopes. He is visiting
Professor of Astrophysics at the California Institute of
Technology.

His other publications include *The Nature of the Universe*
(1950; a Pelican), *A Decade of Decision* (1953), *Frontiers of
Astronomy* (1956), *Of Men and Galaxies* (1965), and *Man
in the Universe* (1966). His other novels are *The Black
Cloud* (1957), *Ossian's Ride* (1959), *Fifth Planet* (1963;
with G. Hoyle), *Seven Steps to the Sun* (1970; with
G. Hoyle), *The Molecule Men* (1971; with G. Hoyle) and
The Inferno (1973). Fred Hoyle, who expresses himself at
one and the same time with the precision of a scientist
and the bluntness of a Yorkshireman, has also published a
play, *Rockets in Ursa Major* (1962), and is the joint author
of *A for Andromeda* (1962). He was knighted in 1972.

Fred Hoyle

October the First is Too Late

Penguin Books

Penguin Books Ltd, Harmondsworth,
Middlesex, England
Penguin Books Inc., 7110 Ambassador Road,
Baltimore, Maryland 21207, U.S.A.
Penguin Books Australia Ltd, Ringwood,
Victoria, Australia
Penguin Books Canada Ltd, 41 Steelcase Road West,
Markham, Ontario, Canada
Penguin Books (N.Z.) Ltd, 182-190 Wairau Road,
Auckland 10, New Zealand

First published by William Heinemann Ltd, 1966
Published in Penguin Books 1968
Reprinted 1971, 1973, 1974, 1975, 1976

Made and printed in Great Britain by
Richard Clay (The Chaucer Press), Ltd,
Bungay, Suffolk
Set in Linotype Times

To the Reader

The 'science' in this book is mostly
scaffolding for the story, story-telling in
the traditional sense. However, the discussions
of the significance of time and of the
meaning of consciousness are intended to be
quite serious, as also are the contents of
chapter fourteen.

Fred Hoyle, 14 July 1965

1 Prelude

I had been invited to compose a piece for the Festival of Contemporary Music, Cologne, 1966. My intention was a set of variations in serial form. I chose the serial formula, partly as a technical exercise, partly because I had a fancy to end each variation with the sound of a farmyard animal.

The first three variations went smoothly enough but I got stuck on the fourth. I decided a change of air was needed to get me out of the rut. My decision to go for a week down to Cornwall was the trifling beginning of a sequence of momentous events. It was as if I had crossed a more or less flat watershed that nevertheless separates rivers flowing to quite different oceans.

I was lying on the clifftops in the sunshine trying to puzzle out exactly how one might imitate the whinny of a horse. I must have dozed off to sleep for perhaps ten minutes. I woke with a tremendous tune, the melody of a lifetime, running in my head. It flowed on and on, statement and response, question and answer, seemingly without end. It began with a series of rocking chords in the bass. Then the first phrase came in the treble. From there on it took off with a momentum that never seemed to die, the kind of *perpetuum mobile* you get in the first movement of the sixth Brandenburg concerto. Quickly, I scribbled the cascade of notes on a piece of score paper, for this was not a case in which I dare trust to memory. How inevitable a melody is while you have it running in your head, how difficult to recapture once it has gone.

On the way back to my lodging at a local farmhouse I passed several horses grazing but the thought of my fourth variation was gone now. Late into the night I pondered on the ramifications of that tune. It is rare indeed for a long melody to go well with harmony. To produce striking orchestral effects one normally uses a mixture of several scraps of melody, mere fragments. But this case seemed different. Orchestral ideas grew naturally around it. The instruments thundered in my head, their individual qualities, their distinctive tones, became ever more clear, ever sharper. The people of the farm must have thought me a queer fish, I dare say. I sat all day writing for the fever of creation was on me. By the end of the week the piece was essentially finished. There was still routine work to do but nothing more.

I was already on my way back to London before the problem of the Festival recurred to me. It was obvious the variations would never be finished in time. It wasn't just a week that was lost. In the past few days I had burnt up a couple of months of normal effort. I wondered about using the new piece. Reason told me no, emotion told me yes. I desperately wanted to hear the new sounds from the orchestra. I had given it everything, maximum sonority. Yet this was exactly where I would run into trouble. A considerable quantity of electronic music would quite certainly be played. My piece, coming late in the programme, would unfortunately look like an all-out attack on other composers. When compared with the full blast of the true orchestra, their stuff would inevitably sound thin and wan.

Then there were two points of conscience. I don't have any rooted objection to the *avant garde*. While the new fashions have nothing very great to recommend them, they do at least contribute *something* to music. Classical methods work wonderfully well for the positive emotions, for sentiments of epic proportions. But the less pleasant emotions cannot be described at all in classical terms. It was beyond the resources of even the greatest of the old musicians to display genuine anger for instance. So really I had no quarrel with modern styles as such. My quarrel was with a fashion that claimed those styles to be everything, as if a craftsman were to insist on always working with a single tool.

My second worry was whether my piece could really be described as 'contemporary'. Of course it was contemporary in the sense that it was recent, not more than a week old, but there is a sense in which the word represents form and technique rather than chronology.

The choice evidently lay between withdrawing and going ahead with the new piece. After something of a struggle with myself I decided to go ahead. There was a lot to be done, parts to be copied, and then mailed way to Germany. The orchestra was to be the Mannheim Symphony.

The journey to Cologne was uneventful. Two rehearsals were scheduled for me. After a few misunderstandings I managed to get the playing into tolerable shape. My time was an evening of the second week. As it came round I was motivated in the following way. My thoughts on the piece had dulled in the intervening weeks but the sound of the orchestra reawakened something of the fury I had felt in that week in Cornwall. This, and the fact that several people had heard my rehearsals and had already spread critical rumours, put me in a combative state of mind by the time I walked on to the platform to conduct.

All worries disappeared at the first surge of the music. For the next seventeen minutes I was totally committed to the vision I had had on those faraway Cornish cliffs. In rehearsal I deliberately held the orchestra back. When an orchestra becomes excited with a new work it is good policy to wait until the first actual performance before giving them their full head. I not only gave it them now I drove them with an intensity I had never shown before. In a sense it comes ill of a composer to speak well of his own work; but it is all so far back now that I think I can be reasonably objective. As the melody surged into the final fanfare I knew I had in no way disgraced myself. I also knew I had contributed little to music except a stirring fifteen minutes or so. The musician's problem is stated very simply: how to display the more worthwhile aspects of human nature differently from the old masters. Modern styles have concentrated in part on the meaner side of things, as I have already remarked, in part on the purely abstract. Modern styles are no solution to the problem but neither was my piece. It was an extrapolation of the old methods. It faced the challenge of comparison with the composers of the past – for fifteen minutes. It pointed no way to anybody else.

This criticism I would have been entirely willing to accept if the audience had admitted the straightforward merit of what had been done. They didn't. There was scattered applause mixed with boos and hisses. Momentarily nonplussed I failed to take a quick bow and to make a quick exit. The hissing increased. Suddenly I became coldly angry. With an imperious

9

gesture I turned to the leader and shouted loudly, 'Bar one!' Such is the respect of a German orchestra for its conductor that the players all obediently turned back to the beginning. Before anybody in the audience realized what was going to happen the rolling bass chords started again. The shouting behind me held its own for a little while until the orchestra picked up volume. Then as the full chords broke loose the mob amounted to little more than a whisper in a storm. At the end they had their say, or rather their shout. This time it was quite full blooded. I was in no doubt of what to do. I bowed around the hall twice, shook the leader's hand, patted him on the shoulder, and walked out.

As I made my way back to the hostel I fully intended to quit Cologne the following morning. Yet when morning came I saw no reason to run away like a whipped dog. I found it much easier to behave normally, as if nothing had happened, than I would have expected. My fellow musicians were only meeting me in small numbers at a time now. Perhaps for this reason they had lost something of the confidence of the evening before. Several of the critics went out of their way to tell me, more or less out of the back of the hand, how much they had enjoyed my piece. Well, well. I remembered being told, as a youngster, that if universal approbation represented a hundred per cent on a scale of appreciation, then to be universally well known, but disliked, was already worth fifty per cent. To be entirely unknown corresponded to the zero mark.

I did leave the Festival two days before its end, not under any compulsion, but because I got bored. Two weeks of cater-wauling was more than I could take. So midway through the afternoon I found myself at the airport. It chanced that Alex Hamilton had decided to get out too. We travelled back together. Alex is the untypical Scot. He has a remarkable gift for floating through life. His musical style is modern, abstract, technically very good. His great gift, outside music, lies in avoiding doing the things he doesn't want to do. He couldn't understand why I had gone so deliberately out of my way to make trouble for myself. He didn't criticize me directly. We sat together, Alex making lighter conversation than I was able to do myself. Every now and then he would stop talking and begin shaking with silent laughter. I stood it as long as I could and then said, 'I'm glad you think it funny.' It wasn't a very

10

worthwhile remark but it sent him into still more violent contortions. Then he patted me on the shoulder and said, 'It was marvellous, just marvellous.'

We got into London airport more or less on time. Quickly we were into the reception hall and through immigration. Then came an unconscionably long wait in the customs hall. If the trend towards faster aircraft goes on long enough we shall end up by taking more time to unload the baggage than for the flight, I thought grumpily. A sudden slap on the back caused me to turn sharply, a cross look still on my face. It was a slim dark-haired man in his early thirties. Recognition came in perhaps half a second. 'Thank goodness it's you,' he said, 'for a second I thought I might have slapped the wrong back.'

It was John Sinclair. We'd been at school together. We had won scholarships to Cambridge in the same year, his in mathematics, mine in music. Besides his mathematics Sinclair had a natural liking for music. In our university days I was as much interested in the piano itself as in composition. The larger part of my musical education I got outside the lecture-room, by playing great quantities of music. I developed in those days the habit of riding through a composer's works totally, symphonies, quartets, as well as straight piano music. John Sinclair used to spend many a spare hour in my rooms.

We were both interested in mountains. Already at school we had been out on one or two walking tours together. We kept it going at university. At the end of our third year we made a great trip to Skye. A party of four of us camped in Glen Brittle. We had a magnificent couple of weeks climbing in the Cuillin. The penultimate day was very wet. We spent it in the tents, cooking and talking. Our talk centred on what we were going to do the following year. Sinclair and I came to the tentative conclusion that we'd make a trip to the remarkable sandstone mountains of the extreme north-west. This plan never came to fruition. I won a scholarship to Italy in the following year. By the time I returned Sinclair was away in the United States. Although we had only met twice in the intervening years I had followed his career with more than a passing interest. The Royal Society just managed to scramble him into its Fellowship, at the age of twenty-nine, in time to forestall the award of a Nobel Prize. I followed what was going on as best I could in magazines like the *New Scientist* and the

11

Scientific American. I knew he had contributed a decisive step in the physics of elementary particles, something of a highly algebraic nature.

I made the introductions.

'Where are you in from?'

'New York. And you?'

'We're just back from Cologne. Music Festival.'

Our bags came at last. Alex and I checked them through customs. I said to him, 'Let's wait.' It was some minutes before Sinclair joined us. 'How about a taxi into town, and having dinner together?' he said. This was fine by me. I'd been a little shy suggesting it. When you haven't seen a man for six years, when he's gone a long way in those six years, you never know exactly where you stand. But it seemed that John hadn't changed much, in spite of his towering success. He was thinner now than he used to be, and I would have said he'd got a slightly worried look about him. We took a taxi to my place, ostensibly for a drink. We had several drinks.

Dinner began to seem less important. Alex had developed quite a sway. He sat firmly down in the largest chair, gave a flowing gesture, with the hand that was not holding a glass, and said, 'Music.'

'What? Any preferences, anybody?'

'Anything, anything you like.' He turned to John, 'We don't have preferences, do we? What we want is, music!'

I had not the slightest idea of what was going to come out as my hands came down on the keyboard. It was a Chopin nocturne, one I couldn't recall having played for years. True I used to go quite a lot for Chopin in my late teens. Quite a bit has been written on the techniques of seduction. My not very humble submission is that most of such stuff is plain nonsense. For every girl of eighteen who can be broken down by feats of muscle power on the football field there are ten who will swoon into your arms at the sound of a Chopin waltz or mazurka. I have no doubt the same system works just as well at later ages, but for me at least it had come to seem too cheap and easy. Seducing a girl with your own music is all fair and aboveboard. Doing it with someone else's had come to seem not quite proper, like shooting a sitting bird, or fishing with maggots. Anyway, out came the nocturne, somewhere from my subconscious memory. The alcohol stopped any worries about forgetting the way it went. As the piece glided to its end I had the feeling I had never played Chopin more perfectly. No doubt this was the effect of the alcohol too. Yet it is a mistake to think in terms of absolutes. It's the way you feel, the way your audience feels, that really counts. Alex was getting quite high now, 'More Choppy, please. More Choppy.'

They kept me at it for two solid hours. Whenever I tried to leave the stool Alex would have none of it. 'Keep playing,' he yodelled. Where the stuff came from I simply couldn't say. It just seemed to well up in the fingers. There was a great mazurka. I couldn't even remember its number. The notes came unbidden. I began a piece which at first I couldn't place. Then I realized this was the calm beginning of the tremendous polonaise-fantaisie. For a while I had fears I could never remember the magnificent second half. Then I began to listen intently to the music itself. I became lost in it. Not until my fingers came down on the final crashing chord was I aware of any passage of time. They were both on my shoulder now. For a moment I thought Alex was going to weep. I jumped up and said firmly, 'Time for food.'

There were eggs in the refrigerator. Within twenty minutes we had a big omelette all piping hot on the table. John and I ate while Alex talked, his mouth full the whole while. Somehow it sounded very witty. Wit, like love, evidently lies in the ear of the listener. We had some fresh fruit. Then I went off to make coffee.

When I came back Alex was nowhere to be seen.

'He's gone, apparently.'

That was Alex all over. He had the gift of appearing out of nowhere and of disappearing without the slightest explanation. He was the nearest human embodiment of the Cheshire cat I had ever met.

'Has he really gone?' asked John.

'Oh yes. He never goes in any other way.'

'What an odd fellow. Well, Dick, how have you been these last few years?'

Perhaps I should explain that I was christened Richard and that my nose, broken in a boyhood accident, somehow dominates my appearance. With this formality out of the way, let me return to my story.

We settled ourselves comfortably as we drank our coffee.

13

The conversation turned naturally on memories and anecdotes of our earlier years. No third person would have been much interested in the talk. By the time we had done it was half past one. I didn't know where John had been intending to stay the night but it was obvious that he should occupy my spare room. I got out towels and bed linen. Half an hour later I was asleep, blissfully unaware of the strange events that even the near future was to reveal.

2   Fugue

We were nearly through breakfast the following morning when John said, 'How about it?'

'How about what?'

'The trip we once planned to the north-west. Liathach, An Teallach, Suilven, and the rest of 'em.'

'When?'

'As soon as you're ready.'

'I'm ready now. What shall we go in?'

'I can borrow a car easily enough.'

'That wasn't what I was thinking. This time of year the hotels in the Highlands are certain to be full.'

John thought about this for a minute and got up from the table. 'I'll see what I can do. Where's the phone?'

It was half an hour before he reappeared. 'Well, it's all fixed.'

'What?'

'I've got hold of a caravan with a car to pull it.'

It wasn't a very great achievement, not for a Nobel laureate, but he seemed quite proud of it.

After breakfast John went out, took a taxi, and disappeared. I set about cleaning up. I telephoned a few people to say I would be away for about ten days. Then I searched for my boots and other items of mountain equipment. The boots looked just about serviceable. I hadn't kept them as carefully as they deserved. Rucksack, a bit of rope, anorak, socks, breeches, I scattered them over the floor. I packed and was ready when John returned. It was nearly one o'clock by the time we headed our outfit through St John's Wood on to the A1.

The journey to the north became an unmitigated bore. It was dark when we reached Scotch Corner. We turned off the fast highway, taking the smaller·cross-country road to Penrith. By the time we reached Brough we had both had enough. So we drove away on the moorland road which leads from Brough to

Middleton. It was certain there would be patches of open ground on which we could park the caravan for the night. So it proved, after we had climbed up towards the moors for maybe a couple of miles. We ate a simple but ample meal from provisions we had bought on the way. A mug of tea each, with a big dollop of rum in it, was the last manoeuvre before getting down into our bags.

There was a good deal of rain in the night, so we had no great hopes for the weather the following morning. But when I put on the kettle at about six o'clock it didn't look too bad. Although there was mist on the high ground it seemed as if the rain might hold off. I woke John with a cup of tea and asked him how he would feel about stretching his legs. He said that would be fine, so I cooked about six slices of bacon. Instead of eating it there and then we wrapped it in a piece of aluminium foil. This, a knife, a loaf of bread, and a hunk of cake, went into a rucksack. By a quarter to seven we were away. We took the car along the road until John, who was studying the map, announced that the point of attack had been reached. We laughed at the thought of an attack on Mickle Fell. Yet we knew, gentle as the hill might be so far as height was concerned, there would be plenty of really hard walking before we reached the top. Hard because the ground was broken by big tussocks and by peat hags. The mist wouldn't make navigating easy.

We made the top of a little ridge. The line ahead didn't look right to John. It was characteristic of him that he wouldn't move on until we had fixed the exact point where we were now standing. It was pretty damp. I began to grow cold as we argued. At last we had the contours on the map fitted correctly to the mile or so of country we could see ahead. It was now clear what the trouble was. We hadn't started at quite the point we intended. We had left the car almost a mile short of the right spot. John grumbled to himself, to the effect that he must be losing his grip. Next we got into an argument about which was the best line to take, not so much from a point of view of arriving at the top, but of avoiding the worst of the broken ground. We decided to move leftward in order to avoid the green soggy depression below us. After about half an hour we came on a wire fence that seemed to lead in the right direction. Looking at the map it occurred to me that it might mark the boundary between Westmorland and Yorkshire. If it did it would lead us to exactly where we wanted to be. The time seemed about right for breakfast. We cut two or three slices of bread, munched up the bacon, and started off again, each with a lump of cake in his hand.

We made good progress along the fence because the ground was somewhat smoother along its line than it was in open country. About eight o'clock the mists lifted. Mickle Fell was dead ahead of us. Now it was only a simple walk to the top. As soon as we were on the limestone, or what seemed to be limestone, there was a delightful change of vegetation. Gone was the acid peat bog. Now we had grass beneath our feet and sheep were grazing on the long back of the fell. We made quick progress to the east down a longish ridge to a mine perched near a lake under the hillside. By eleven o'clock we were on the road again.

We were anxious to continue our journey to the north as soon as possible. It was nearly three miles back to the car, the best part of an hour's walk, so we decided to try to get a lift from a passing motorist. Because there wasn't too much traffic, and because most cars might only have room for one of us, we split up. I went about four hundred yards ahead, climbed up a steep little bank and lay out on its top, leaving John to deal with the motorists. Within ten minutes he had a lift. He gave a triumphant wave as the car passed by. We had been wise for there certainly wasn't room in it for me.

The minutes lengthened to half an hour. Every so often a car came around a corner in the road about two hundred yards ahead of my little bank. I could hear them before they came into view. Each one I expected to be ours. An hour went by and still no sign of John. Obviously our borrowed car had failed to start. There was nothing for it but to walk after all. As I stumped the hard road I wished I had not given John my rucksack, not because it was heavy, but because I could have changed into rubbers and then I could have trotted the distance in twenty minutes or so.

The car was there, exactly as we had left it. John was not to be seen, plainly he had gone for help, probably to a garage in Brough. I sat down to wait and another hour went by. What the hell was going on? Why hadn't John left a note, or left the keys so that at least I could get into the damned car? I began

17

to curse these impractical scientists. Reluctantly I set off to walk the further mile to the caravan. John had the key to that too but we had left a window open and I managed to climb in without much trouble. Thereafter, I washed and tried to soothe my nerves with a big pot of tea and a further chunk of cake.

But this wasn't funny any more. By three o'clock I was striding my way into Brough in a high old temper. I found two garages and drew a blank at both. It was another hour before I could persuade a mechanic to drive me to our car. He somehow opened it and soon had the engine going. I paid him £1 and he drove away plainly thinking I was daft. What to do now? I had heard of motorists in the United States who gave a lift and then beat up and robbed their unsuspecting passenger but I could recall no such case in Britain. Yet something like this must have happened. I drove to the place where we had come down off the ridge of Mickle Fell, then back again the whole six miles to Brough, very slowly. At that stage I reported the whole business to a police sergeant. He took it all down in a grave manner which I suspected to be routine. He asked where I was staying and I told him the position of the caravan up on the moor. The police, he said, would get on to the matter immediately and someone would come up to the caravan as soon as they had any information.

There was nothing to be done now but drive back to the van. It was coming up to six o'clock by the time I got there. I was in two minds about cooking dinner. Underneath I was hungry but the worry of the situation dulled my appetite. I decided to stretch out on a bunk for half an hour or so before starting preparations for a meal. As far as I was aware this was exactly what I did. It wasn't until I had eaten and washed up that I saw from my watch it was already nine o'clock. Shortly after, there came a powerful knock at the van door.

It was an inspector in plain clothes, from which I guessed this had become a C I D matter. He asked me a lot of questions about myself. They were not taking John's disappearance lightly now. His reputation as a scientist would in itself have forced them to take it seriously but I suspected there might also be a security aspect to the matter. Hence the questions about myself. I guessed the police wanted to satisfy themselves that I had no part in the business, whatever it was. After about an hour of the questioning the man prepared to leave. I remembered to check my watch with his before he did so. There was nothing wrong with it.

Darkness came on and I settled down for the night. If I had been thoroughly fit I suppose I would quickly have fallen asleep. Now I tossed around uneasily wondering about John Sinclair. Of course I didn't know much about him as he was now, only as he used to be. It certainly seemed as if the intervening years had never existed. We had resumed the old free and easy days of school and university. Yet the intervening years were real enough. John's life must have become more complicated, professionally and socially, than it was when I knew him. To me he might seem the same person but to the world at large this would not be so. These speculations, sensible enough in themselves, got me nowhere.

Suddenly my attention was caught by approaching footsteps. I wriggled out of my bag, found a box of matches and started to light the little gas lamp over the kitchen stove. I was still fumbling when the door opened. Then the light came on and I saw it was John, his face not a foot from mine. The slightly worried look, which I had already remarked the first evening, was more obvious now.

'Where in the hell have you been?' I asked.

He came into the van, slumped on to his bunk, and began to unlace his boots.

'I haven't the slightest idea, Dick. That's the truth.'

It was my impulse to press the matter further. But if what John said was indeed true, if he really had no idea what had happened, it was pointless to argue. Probably it was some kind of blackout. I didn't know whether he had become subject to temporary losses of memory but it was at least a possible explanation. Hard exercise, taken suddenly without any previous training, might have brought on some kind of attack. Anyway he was safe, which was the main thing.

'Hungry?'

'Devilishly so.'

I had a feeling that what he wanted was silence and food. I wasn't averse to another snack myself. With an impressive display of energy I had the table set. Wild and wonderful smells pervaded the caravan within a few minutes. John ate more or less silently. I had a big mug of tea and a piece of cake. I told John about the police. With his agreement I drove to a phone box about half a mile down the road. I put through a 999 call telling the constable on duty that John had turned up and that he seemed to have suffered a temporary amnesia but was quite recovered now. When I returned to the caravan I found him in a deep sleep.

We were very late up the following morning. Partly for this reason, and partly because we had another visit from the inspector, it was on midday before we resumed our journey to the north. What was said between John and the inspector I do not know. They went off for a walk together, returning after about an hour, an hour which I spent cleaning up the van. At all events the inspector seemed satisfied now, which was all that seemed to matter.

We took the outfit straight through the centre of Glasgow. Because we were slow-moving this was probably the quickest way. We managed to find the road to Loch Lomond without much difficulty. We passed various camping sites intent on reaching Glencoe if we possibly could. It seemed a long pull up to Crianlarich and the distance to Tyndrum was somewhat longer than I remembered it. Then we were out on to the beginning of Rannoch Moor. John who was driving muttered something about the caravan being wrong. The outfit began to weave rather violently. He brought it to a quick halt. Inspection showed a puncture on the nearside back wheel of the car. As we got out the jack and spare wheel clouds of midges descended on us in their thousands. We were back in Scotland. It took less than a quarter of an hour to change that wheel. Yet we were practically eaten alive.

We had been fighting time to get to Glencoe in the light. I knew the exact spot where I wanted to go, on to the old road which crosses the new road about two miles the other side of Kingshouse Inn. By the time we reached the place the last of the light was gone. It was impossible to execute any complicated movement with the caravan. All we could do was simply drive straight ahead on to the old road. This meant the caravan would be the wrong way round for making an exit. We would have to turn it by hand. Worse, the car was wedged in on the wrong side. After uncoupling, there was no possibility, because of the narrowness of the road, the unsurfaced old road, of getting it back on to the highway. We would need the car itself the following morning to drive about four miles down the glen to the beginning of the ordinary route up Bidean nam Bian. Sufficient unto the day is the evil thereof.

We were early astir. After a quick cup of tea, cooking bacon, packing the rucksack, it was still only 6 a.m. by the time we were ready to be off. The morning was perfect, not a cloud in the sky. But now we had to tackle the problem of the car. The simplest solution seemed to be to continue along the old road, for the best part of a mile, until it joined the surfaced road again. We took it very slowly indeed. Even so it was a wild ride. This was an occasion for a jeep or a Land-Rover. There was a good deal of scraping of the undercarriage but finally we made it without incurring disaster. Ten minutes later we had parked near the rather gloomy Loch Triochtan.

The track up the mountainside appeared unpleasantly steep. Yet once we made a start it turned out to be not as bad as it looked. We followed the bed of a stream for quite a way up a little valley which lay back into the mountain more than we had expected. After maybe a mile we decided to cut out of the stream bed, up to the left. Once again the slope was not too bad. By eight o'clock we reached a little corrie which I guessed to be about a thousand feet below the summit. Ahead of us was a fine rock buttress, presumably the famous Churchdoor Buttress. In the floor of the corrie there were wonderful pools of clear cold water. It was now quite warm and we spent a good half-hour over a leisurely breakfast. For the first time we appreciated the advantages of the caravan. It was much to be preferred to a tent because of the midges. It was to be preferred to an hotel because of the wonderful early start we could make from it. Down in the hotel at Kingshouse, or at Ballachulish, we should only just now be sitting down to breakfast. It was true we *were* having breakfast, but at nearly three thousand feet, with most of the day's climbing already done.

We were off again just before nine o'clock, on to a rather loose slope of scree and broken rocks. It took us up for about five hundred feet. Then we were on the summit ridge in bright sunshine. The rocks here were firm and warm. We mounted quickly to the top. It was going to be hot and a haze was already rising. To the north the Mamores and Ben Nevis looked tremendous. To the south were the ragged peaks of Glen Etive. We had no need of hurry, we spent a good hour on the top. In my capacity as quartermaster I produced my *bonne bouche*, two tins of orange juice. Then we set off along the ridge at a steady easy pace. We went just as we felt like it, down the long shelving ridge towards Glen Etive, then up again to the beginning of the Beinn Fhada ridge. Then down a steepish short slope, up again over a couple of bumps or so, to a little col. Here our route lay down a steep, broken hillside on the left. There was roughly a thousand feet of it and it didn't look inviting, to untrained men. We had a friendly disagreement as to which was the best way down. John chose a gully between rocky walls, a kind of stone shoot. I thought the more open ground to the right would be better. When I had gone down it for perhaps a hundred feet I realized I was mistaken. As I struggled downward I lost contact with John. When I next saw him he was a long way below me, maybe two or three hundred feet. I stuck at it and at last came to where he was lying resting on a boulder. I suggested we keep going down the widish scoop that lay on our right, that it would take us down to the stream in the big corrie into which we were descending. John laughed. He asserted the scoop would take us down to a cliff edge. I couldn't see how he knew this but after my mistake on the slope above I didn't think it wise to argue.

The bottom of the corrie was an amazing affair. It looked as though it was going to be a flat bottom. Then at the last moment the hillside plunged steeply into a little gorge. The gorge ran for more than a mile along what looked like a flat valley. This was the hidden valley I had heard of many times. Whether by luck, instinct, or sheer skill, I don't know, but John led the way to a point where there was an easy breach in the cliffs where we could get down to the stream and to its opposite side on which we could see a good track.

I was hot with the ridge walk and and the steep descent. I suggested we have a bathe in the stream. The idea took on. Within five minutes I was down into one of the clear pools. Being cold is a strange experience when you come to think about it. Being really cold is unpleasant but it isn't a sharp agonizing business. Cold is a stealthy, unrelenting enemy. The only pleasurable aspect of it, to my knowledge, is when you come piping hot down a mountainside and jump into a pool of icy water. The pleasure lasts no more than thirty seconds. You stick it for another minute and then out you crawl as fast as you can. This was exactly what we did. It was while we were drying off in the sunshine that the odd thing struck me. Back at school we had often stripped our shirts off after football. I knew perfectly well John had a strawberry birthmark, about the size of a half-crown, in the small of his back. There was now no trace of it.

3 Intermezzo

Birthmarks and suchlike, 'marks prodigious' as the old wizard of Stratford had it, aren't quite the stuff of polite conversation. Back at school I would not have had the least inhibition. Now it took some effort.

'Hey, John, didn't you have a birthmark in the middle of your back?'

'Yes, of course. What of it?'

'Well, it isn't there any more.'

'Of course it's there.'

'I assure you it isn't.'

'Must be the strong sunshine. There's no contrast out here.'

We made our way to the throat of the valley. There was an amazing tangle of great boulders. Threading our way through them we came to easy slopes of grass that led down into Glencoe itself. When we were back in camp I put the kettle on for the much needed cup of tea.

John said, 'You'd better check that mark.'

I had been right. There wasn't the least trace of it. Foolishly, I said, 'You haven't had it removed or anything?'

'Of course I haven't.'

John made no further comment. His face was knit in a tense expression, one I had seen often enough before when he was engaged on some awkward problem. I knew better than to ask him to explain. He scribbled on a big scratch pad as we drank our tea.

I left him at it and drove down the valley to the sea. I took the left fork towards Port Appin. I didn't quite know what to make of John and his troubles so I put them out of my mind as best I could. I began wondering about the possibilities of a sea symphony. It was certainly an idea but perhaps not a very good one. There is of course great beauty and drama in the sea. Yet the subject is unattractively amorphous, far removed from human problems. In a way it seemed just an escape formula, an excuse for a display of flashing orchestral effects. I doubted whether there was much more scope in this direction.

It was half past six when I returned to the van. John was still figuring. I poured both of us a generous woof of a drink. By the time we were through it I said we'd better be off to the hotel at Ballachulish unless he was keen to cook the dinner.

'Let's go then. I want to use the phone.'

I hadn't expected the hotel to be so full. With mild apprehension I asked if they could manage dinner for the two of us. A woman said she would see and would we like a drink in the meantime? We had the drink and the woman came back. Yes, they could manage dinner but we'd have to wait until about a quarter past eight.

'I'll do my phoning now,' grunted John when she'd gone.

He left me in a milling crowd, apparently talking for the most part about their experiences on the road. There seemed not the slightest appreciation of the magic of a wonderful day spent in one of the most beautiful places on Earth. At half past seven somebody started bashing away at a gong. All but three or four of the company drifted out of the bar. There was an upright piano along one side of the room. I opened the lid and fingered the keys in an idle fashion. 'Do you play?' asked a middle-aged woman. For answer I pulled up a chair and settled into a number from one of the latest shows. The piano was of the honky-tonk variety which I never can resist. It was gloriously out of tune. I meandered through two or three numbers and they loved it. The woman's husband, or so I took him to be, said, 'Have a drink?' I asked for half a pint of bitter. I was sipping it, making polite conversation, when John returned. I could judge nothing from his face.

At last our turn for dinner came round, none too soon, for I was hungry. We were put at a table by ourselves.

'Any idea of what you want to do tomorrow?' I asked.

'I'm afraid we'll have to call it off, Dick. But don't let me drag you back to London.'

'Is there anything I can do?'

'Not explicitly. How are you fixed?'

'In what way?'

'Have you any engagements, ones it would be difficult to break?'

'Not really. Why?'

'I'll have to go back to the States. If you're free I'd like you to come along.'

I laughed. My bank manager was just going to love the suggestion. 'What would I use for money?'

'There's no problem. You travel on contract.'

We closed the subject at this point until we were back in the van. Then John began, 'I suppose I'd better tell you a bit of what's going on. It won't make much sense I'm afraid.'

I put a pile of clothing under my pillow, to make a backrest as I stretched out on my bunk. My legs were beginning to stiffen up.

'I suppose you've followed the general outline of the things that have been turning up in space research?'

'Yes, more or less, so far as it's possible from newspaper reports.'

'One of the aims of the space programme is to take a look at the outside world in unfamiliar parts of the spectrum.'

'You mean things like X-rays and gamma rays?'

'That's right. But of course X-rays and gamma rays are at the high frequency end. There's a lot of stuff in the far infra-red, stuff that gets absorbed in our own atmosphere just like the X-rays do. I'm talking now about wavelengths roughly a hundred times less than the shortest radio waves.'

'What's the point – curiosity?'

'It started that way. The first idea was to pick up radiation from the Sun, to check that it had the intensity everybody expected it to have.'

'Did it?'

'Within a reasonable margin of accuracy. It wasn't something to hold a press conference about. Yet interesting, technically. That was all, or nearly all.'

'It doesn't sound as if it would make the girls swoon.'

'What was odd though was that some of the electronics, not in this experiment itself you understand, but electronics connected with other things that were going on, went badly wrong. It seemed as if they were suffering from pick-up troubles. Naturally there was a hell of an inquest about it. Nothing sensible could be found. All the circumstantial evidence pointed to a modulation in the region of a hundred mega-cycles, a modulation on the current output from the new infra-red experiment. On the face of it this seemed impossible. Well, to cut it short, the lads just had time to modify the gadgetry before the next shot went up. The circumstantial evidence unfortunately turned out to be right. There *was* a modulation at nearly a hundred megacycles.'

'Could it have been a pick-up as well?'

'Everybody felt it had to be. Well, the inquest grew now to major proportions. It was still going on when I left the States. I'm not involved myself very directly with this stuff. It happens the chap in charge of the experiment is a friend of mine. The last thing I heard was that they had a proof it wasn't the Sun itself, at least they thought so. They thought they'd demonstrated it had come from the rocket. Yet nobody had any real idea of why or how.'

'You think it might be the Sun after all?'

I knew how John's mind worked, at any rate psychologically. I had a pretty good notion this was his opinion.

'I don't know – yet. Back at the hotel I put a call through to this friend. I couldn't get him personally but I got one of his chaps. They're going to ring back with some information I need tomorrow morning. Then I'll be in a much better position to say.'

I lay awake that night for a long time. It astonished me how easily John had been able to fall asleep. I could hear him breathing deeply and quite regularly as if there was nothing in the world to worry about. I had a general idea of what he had told me. Yet for the life of me I couldn't see its relevance to the disturbing incidents of the last three days.

The following morning John went back to the hotel. It was half past ten by the time he came back.

'We'll have lunch at twelve. There's a plane from Glasgow to London at three o'clock. We should have time to catch it.'

'How about the car and the caravan?'

'We'll take the car to Glasgow. I've made arrangements for the van to be collected from here.'

'What else?'

'Can you manage the midday plane to New York on Friday?'

This would give me three days to put my affairs to rights in London. It wouldn't be easy but I could make it. 'I suppose so.'

'Good, I'm going to put in an hour's calculation.'

John worked quickly and keenly. I could see it was nothing but algebra and arithmetic. As I watched I was struck by the difference between the mathematician and the musician. When I had worked myself with a similar intensity a few weeks ago, back in Cornwall, I had been in a kind of trance. There was nothing trance-like about John. With a swoop like an eagle he came to a stop. I didn't need to ask him if it had turned out successfully. So much was obvious. Nor did I ask him what it meant.

'Satisfied?'

'Yes.' He sat for a minute and then added, 'Funny.'

'How?'

'The conclusion. I have demonstrated the correctness of a hunch – at the expense of an appalling conclusion. Oddly enough it seems more satisfactory this way round, better than being wrong and having a sensible, straightforward answer. It shows the important thing is to know your reasoning powers work properly. *Where* they lead you is really unimportant, which I suppose is why human beings are able to achieve completely new things. Basically, it's why we're no longer swinging by our tails from trees.'

That was all I got out of him.

The journey back to London was uneventful. We parted at the air terminal, each to make his own arrangements. We didn't meet again until an hour before the plane to New York was due to depart on the Friday morning.

The intervening days were busy enough for me. Actually I must admit that I was quite glad to get out of London. Frankly, I had got my personal affairs into something of a tangle. I managed to track down Alex Hamilton, not an easy exercise. I asked him to keep an eye on my place, to use it if he wanted. I told him a little of my difficulties, lest in occupying my simple apartments he should find himself assailed by too many girls on too many sides. This sent him into another of his prolonged fits of silent laughter. He asked me if I had any spare unwanted cash to lend him. I said emphatically I had not.

We grew mellow in the transatlantic plane after a couple of cocktails. The hours slipped away and John and I soon found ourselves through American immigration and customs.

We took a taxi from Kennedy airport to an hotel whose

name I have forgotten. It was somewhere mid-town. At dinner that night, which we ate in a near-by restaurant, I at last got round to asking John what his plans were. He answered:

'We're going on to California as soon as I'm through the things I must do here. It'll probably take about three days. I think it's simpler if I work it out alone. Do you think you can keep yourself happy for a day or two?'

I said I had no doubt I could find plenty to do. He went on:

'I'm going to turn in pretty early tonight. I find it's a good idea to take the change of clock in at least a couple of bites.'

It may seem strange that until then I had no idea of exactly where we were going. It is my practice in life to take as little account of times and schedules as I can. I like to be as little tied down by commitments. Surprises are the spice of life. Surprises rarely come to those busy fellows who are always consulting their engagement book. As I got into bed that night I had no idea what I was going to do in the next two or three days. It turned out they were quite uneventful. For one thing I felt tired, more exactly, drained of energy, I suppose by the five-hour shift in the clock.

If I had known I should never see New York again, I would have made an effort to do much more in the way of sightseeing during those three days. On the evening of the second day I found a note from John saying we were booked to San Diego on an eleven o'clock flight the following morning and that he would see me at the flight-gate half an hour before take-off.

We were met at San Diego airport by a young man, apparently a graduate student at the university. He drove us north about ten miles to an hotel in La Jolla. We were shown up to our rooms. I decided I was in need of sleep, a wise move in view of the party to which we were apparently invited that night.

I got up at about five o'clock, shaved and dressed, and then took a stroll on the beach. This was my first sight of the Pacific. I was to see much more of it in the days to come. The beach stretched to the north for a mile or so. Beyond were cliffs running into the distance as far as I could see.

A car arrived for me at half past six. The driver introduced himself – I am sorry to say I immediately forgot his name. We chatted without the least trace of embarrassment as he drove up through a complex of small roads on to the side of a steepish hill. It occurred to me that one would never have got into such an immediately casual relationship with anybody back home. We pulled up outside a single-storey house.

John had arrived already. There were one or two women there so it seemed this was to be a social occasion rather than a work conference. But the conference developed all right. If I had been more experienced in the American way of life I would have realized how inevitable this was. Work conferences always develop at every dinner party provided the men have some common interest. We started with drinks, which were enlivened by the arrival of a spritely fellow wearing an incredible hat. It was of the trilby variety. It looked as if it had been treated by being first buried in the ground for a year or two, then by being thrown as food to an army of hungry mice. His name was Art Clementi. I did not forget the name this time.

There seemed plenty to talk about. John was apparently well known in these parts, so drinks took quite a while. They dissolved imperceptibly into a buffet supper. When the women learnt I was a musician there were the usual demands that I should play. Many musicians detest being invited to the piano at times when they feel they should be off duty. I have never developed a hard and fast dividing line between being on and off duty so playing at odd moments never worries me. I rattled off a couple of Scarlatti sonatas. Then a big fellow standing, somewhat unsteadily, a glass in one hand, by the piano, said, 'How about that Tchaikovsky thing?' He hummed a few notes. Evidently he meant the first piano concerto. I threw off the big opening chords and said, rather unkindly, 'Now you do the orchestra.' They all laughed, the big man as well, not in the least embarrassed. So I began the incredible Tchaikovsky Opus 1, No. 1, incredible because it was Tchaikovsky's first work. When I came to the storming finish I heard the big man mutter, 'Christ!'

A few of the people left. The women seemed to melt away, at maybe half past ten. I noticed the time because I was beginning to feel sleepy again, in fact I was wondering how soon we would get away. Apart from John and me there were six of them. I guessed Clementi must be the friend John had spoken about back in Scotland. He wanted to know what had brought us hot-footed from England.

'Because I know where the modulation is coming from.'

'Then just give us a hint,' said the big man.

John was almost irritatingly precise. He took three quite simple diagrams out from his briefcase. On each there were just three lines meeting at a point. On each line there was an arrow, two pointing away from the point of intersection, the other towards it. The angles between the lines were marked.

'We've had three cases where vehicles have changed directions. In each of them I've shown the direction of the Sun, at the moment of change.'

'As seen from the vehicle?'

'Right. Now you'd better check my facts because a lot depends on them.'

Clementi took up the sheets, studied them, then shook his head. 'We could do that tomorrow. I'm sure you'll have it right.' He turned to the others and grinned, giving them a wink.

John went on, 'Everybody believes something in the rocket is at fault, because the frequencies changed when the rocket changed.'

'That seems to settle it.'

'Then why are the frequencies somewhat different in the three cases?'

John pulled out a fourth sheet. On it were four columns, three numbers in each column. He pointed to the first. 'These were the frequencies on the three occasions before the change of direction was made. You see they're not the same. What should cause the difference?'

'I don't know. But for that matter why the hell is there a change whenever the course corrections are made? The mere fact there *are* changes shows there must be a connexion with the rocket.'

'I'm not doubting it. But the connexion is with the direction of the rocket not with the electronics inside it.'

Clementi winked again, not I saw by way of derision but to fire John with a little emotion. He didn't succeed. John went on in the same irritatingly precise fashion, 'I'm sorry it's so triflingly simple. The whole thing turns on the direction of the rocket relative to the Sun. In the second column I've divided the frequencies in the first column by the sine of the corresponding angles. You see the numbers are still different.'

'I'd expect them to be different,' grunted one of the men.

'Then I noticed that if I normalized everything to the speed of the rocket something very interesting happened. The speeds were about twenty per cent different in the three cases. I took one of the three as standard and divided this time by the speeds. These are the numbers in the third column here. They're very nearly identical.'

I didn't understand what all this was about. But I did see, elementary as it all looked, that it produced a sharp reaction in the local boys.

'I did exactly the same for the frequencies measured after the shifts of direction.'

John produced another piece of paper, again with four columns. He pointed to the third and said, 'You see they're the same, not only the same among themselves, but the same as before the changes were made.'

'What's the fourth column for?' asked Clementi.

'The numbers in the fourth column are just a little more nearly equal than those in the third. The difference is very slight. It was a check, a sort of clinching factor.'

'Clinching for what?'

'For the Sun. Those last figures include the Doppler shift correction, the shift due to the rocket motion in the solar direction.'

There was a long silence. Then Clementi nodded gravely, 'That's what I was afraid of, right from the beginning. You're telling us it's the solar radiation itself that's got this modulation on top of it. Granted you haven't gone crazy and cooked the numbers that's certainly what it looks like.'

'What does it look like?' I asked.

Clementi turned on me. 'It looks as if the Sun is emitting a sharply directed beam of infra-red radiation. The modulation was due to our rocket cutting across the interference fringes.'

'But how the hell can the Sun be emitting a directed beam? It's impossible,' burst out one of the men.

'If you'd asked me an hour ago I'd have said it was impossible. But the facts are clear. It's preposterous and outrageous but it must be true.'

I could see John too was beginning to feel tired. He yawned

and stretched himself and said, 'Well, at least there's something to be done.'

'There's a hell of a lot to be done.'

'I can't see any point in having a directed beam of radiation – and this must be fantastically directional – unless it's used for transmitting information.'

'By whom, for God's sake?'

'How the devil should I know. The thing to do next is to look for some intrinsic form of modulation. We've got to filter out this effect of the interference fringes. Then we must look for some genuine source modulation.'

Quite spontaneously everybody began to consume strong drinks at a very rapid rate. In spite of their comparative reticence, John's disclosures, simple as they might be, had produced a profound sense of shock. I didn't understand what had been said with any great clarity so I suppose things weren't as sharp to me as they were to the others. Yet I gathered that someone, or something, was using the Sun as a signalling device.

4 Tempo di Minuetto

I lay awake for a little while that night. A remarkable conclusion had obviously been pieced together from the simplest
fragments, like a crushing position in a chess game built by a
master from a series of seemingly trifling moves. It was the
pattern, the sequence, that really counted, not the intrinsic
difficulty of any particular step. The data John had used were
no doubt well known to hundreds of people, if not to thousands, but the relevant facts had been embedded in a million-
and-one irrelevancies.

No doubt entirely due to chance I had become involved in a
tremendous situation. It hardly needed special knowledge to
understand the implication of what I had heard. Every single
one of the men involved in tonight's discussion had sought an
alibi, either in understatement or in flippancy. They were
trying to avoid the significance of the situation. Not of course
permanently but to get themselves used to it by slow stages.

The following day I received a cheque for $1,500, paid on
account, through the University of California. I turned it
straightaway into travellers' cheques. I hired a car from a local
agency. The next two days I spent driving along the coast and
into the back country. Possession of the car gave me a new
dimension of freedom. The effects of the journey, particularly
of the time switch, were passing off now. In short I was beginning to enjoy myself.

On the third day I was asked to present myself at ten-thirty
the following morning at such-and-such a building on the
university campus. I was shown to a pleasant office overlooking the sea. It was rather like looking down from the
Cornish cliffs, except the light was stronger here. John came in
with a man of about fifty-five. I was asked to describe exactly
what had happened on our trip to Scotland.

I gave a simple factual account, answered a few questions,
and that was that. John went out with the man. A few minutes
later he returned alone.

'Sorry, Dick, I've been so much occupied. We'll meet for dinner tonight. Not here, in Los Angeles. Let's say half past six. You've got a car?'

I nodded.

He produced a map. 'This is the place here, at the intersection of Wilshire and Santa Monica Boulevards.'

I drove to Los Angeles during the afternoon. It would have been quicker by the inland freeway but I decided to keep on the coast road through Long Beach. I wanted to see the various coastal places I had read about. They didn't live up to my expectations. I was glad by the time I reached Santa Monica.

I wasn't familiar with the district or with the traffic conditions. Yet it was less bewildering than I would have expected. Without too much trouble I reached the restaurant. John was late but not grossly so. Yet to be late at all was unusual for him.

'We'll get away from science for one night,' he said as we sat down at a table, which he had apparently booked beforehand.

'I've been pretty hard at it ever since we got into New York. To be frank I'm damn tired.'

'What's the general pitch?'

'Well, it's obvious we need a new vehicle out there with special instrumentation. There's nothing difficult in it at all. Not experimentally I mean. But it's the devil to get anything unusual done. The whole space programme is going ahead like some enormous juggernaut. Only with the highest priority can you get anything changed.'

'I suppose if you know exactly what you want to do that's the most efficient way.'

'If you know what you want to do, beforehand. Which of course means you're not going to find anything of very much interest.'

'Did you get your way?'

'Yes, with Art's help. We've been up at J P L – the Jet Propulsion Lab all day, arguing. Once they were convinced, everything went smoothly, but they took some convincing.'

'When's it going to happen?'

'More or less immediately. A new vehicle was practically ready for launching. It was designed to go a long way out so it's got pretty sensitive controls. It'll do our job very easily. The problem is to get the right packages ready in time.'

'The right black boxes?'

'Yes. The lads will be working night and day on it. Here's the point as it affects you. We're going to use the big receiving dish out in Hawaii. It's out in the islands because there's not much man-made interference. Would you like a trip?'

I said I'd be delighted to make a trip to Hawaii. Then a waiter bore down on our table with a multitude of dishes.

Conversation was somewhat spasmodic for the next half-hour. The meal, an excellent one, deserved justice.

Over the coffee I asked, 'Is this Hawaii trip a joy ride or is it strictly necessary?'

'Not strictly, if by that you mean absolutely essential. But well worthwhile from my point of view. We'll get the data hot off the line. Art's coming with us. The station on Hawaii is his show.'

'When do we take off?'

'I was planning to travel the day after tomorrow. But there's no reason why you shouldn't go on earlier if you want to. By the way I've got an invitation for tonight.'

'More science?'

'God forbid, I'm in need of a rest. This is a friend of a friend of a friend, out in Beverly Hills. We can always leave early if we get bored.'

'Where are you staying?'

'I've got a motel back in Pasadena. You might as well stay over here by the sea though, it's quite a bit cooler.'

'Then I suppose I'd better find a place before we go to Beverly Hills.'

'Oh, I wouldn't bother. The motels are open all night. You can get one any time. Besides you never know where you'll end up.'

On this remark John paid the bill. We went out to the parking place.

'You'd better follow me, we might as well take both cars. I'm not exactly sure of where to go but I know the general direction.'

I kept faithfully on John's tail through a succession of boulevards and streets. Then we were in a twisting mass of side-roads among large houses. We both came to a halt. John was muttering imprecations. It seemed he was more disturbed by not being able to find the place than he had been by the scientific situation. We started off again. After two more tries we at last drew up outside a prosperous looking domicile. A dozen cars were parked in the roadway outside. Inside, a good-looking woman pressed two large drinks on us, with a welcoming smile, and no questions asked.

We pushed our way into a large room. Perhaps thirty people were in there, talking loudly. I had the impression it would have been possible for almost anybody to have walked in.

In the general bedlam of a cocktail party I am lucky to have something of an advantage over my fellow men. My hearing is abnormally acute so I can still make out what is being said at a stage where the average person is pretty well deafened. I plunged fairly confidently into the morass.

After a quick, not inexpert, survey of the female company a dark-haired girl caught my attention. I thought her face the most interesting of the female element. It was a face of some considerable character. I moved over into her general environment. Because I could just make out what people were trying to say, I soon found a place in the local conversation. The girl I judged to be in her mid-twenties, a few years younger than I was. There came a lull during which a man, who was probably the host, got himself launched into a description of how he had just bought an estate of vast acreage up near Ojai.

I was able to get the dark-haired girl away to myself. Our talk was trivial in the extreme as it was bound to be. I said I was just out from Britain, a simple, not very effective ploy. Her attention became a little warmer, however, when I told her that I was a musician. It seemed I was on the way to Chopin waltzes and mazurkas again.

We were joined by an older, rather handsome woman. The girl drifted away at the first opportunity, perhaps because she was glad to be rescued or because she didn't like the handsome woman. The woman took me on one side, saying confidentially, 'Have you met her before, Lena I mean?'

'No, but I've seen her somewhere I'm sure. Who is she?'

'Do you mean you don't know?'

'Cross my heart.'

'Helena Summers. She was in the film, *The Passionate*.'

'The passionate what?'

The woman laughed, 'No wisecracks.' Then she became still

37

more confidential. Taking my arm she murmured, 'Lena's in bad shape, plenty trouble there.'

There was no opportunity to ask what the plenty trouble was because a handsome, virile man of about my own age suddenly held the stage. I had seen him before so I was pretty sure he must be in the acting world too. He not only had the attention of the others, he had mine too. Astonishingly, he was talking about the effect of Chopin waltzes on young women.

There were two open pianos back-to-back at one end of the big room. The man began to look through a pile of music evidently with the intention of playing himself. I was becoming combative now, rather like a dog whose territory has been infringed. He started on the big Chopin waltz in A flat Major. The interpretation was quite good, the technique somewhat faulty. I found myself appreciably irritated to see the women crowding around the piano.

Then I had the good sense to feel rather ashamed. After all, a lot of practice was needed to play as well as that, which showed my handsome friend must have a very genuine affection for music. Yet I found it difficult not to be jaundiced by the way he switched in a flash to Beethoven's short E Minor sonata. I resisted entering the discussion that followed. But then the girl Lena broke in with the remark that I was a musician. So I was thrown into the pool. I was introduced to the man. His name, Roger Berard, was just about as vaguely familiar as his face. I did my best to pretend to know it well for anything less would have seemed impolite.

'How about playing four hands? Mozart?'

I said that would be excellent. But they couldn't find the right music. Berard picked up the score of Mozart's K488 concerto. 'Do you think we could manage this?' he asked.

I said we'd have to use both pianos.

Two experts with an understanding between them could have managed on one piano. We would have got ourselves into a hopeless tangle of hands and feet.

'There's only one copy. You haven't got another?' my partner asked the man I had guessed to be the host. 'Why the hell should I keep two. I can't even play one.' This brought a chorus of after-dinner laughter.

'We can use both pianos,' I said. 'If you take the solo part, I think I can manage the orchestration.' This was more vicious

38

than it may sound. I knew Berard was in a show-off mood. I suspected he was interested in one of the girls, not apparently the dark girl. By choosing the orchestral accompaniment I naturally had the heavier part. Besides, this was the music I cut my teeth on.

It went as I had expected up to a point. I omitted the orchestral introduction, letting him lead off with the solo part. He began aggressively but with the volume of tone I was able to roll out it must soon have become clear that there was no profit at all for him in a competition. About half-way through the first movement he stopped the nonsense. He began to listen to what he was playing. Then the whole thing went off reasonably well. On a concert platform a four-hands performance is never very attractive. Yet under casual circumstances like this it can be quite exciting, especially if it is unrehearsed. Nobody minds the hesitations and misunderstandings between the two players. It all adds to the fun. We were pressed to continue.

Surprisingly, Berard wanted me to play solo. He got out a volume of Beethoven sonatas talking avidly the while about the late ones. His instinct for music was genuine enough. I saw the artificiality of his earlier remarks really came from the society in which he was living. The world is full of frustrated musicians, people who would have liked to be musicians but who by ill chance had been forced into some other profession. I've met scores of them. They have one characteristic in common. By not being musicians they've done far better for themselves in all material respects than they'd have done as musicians.

I played the Opus 111. There wasn't a great deal of applause at the end but the warmth was obvious. They spoke now in quiet voices, not at all like the uproar that had been going on when John and I came in earlier. It was clear they wanted me to go on but it wasn't easy to think of anything to play after the Opus 111. Almost idly I rattled off the waltz theme of the Diabelli variations. Then I was into the variations proper. There was no turning back now. Once again my memory, or perhaps the thought of the dark girl with plenty trouble, served me well. I got through to No. 33 with a sprinkling of wrong notes but without serious mishap. It was more than enough. They were overwhelmed, crushed. Well they might be. Given the slightest musical sense it is impossible not to be staggered emotionally by the greatest works played at close range. This was the way, at close range, in which the old composers intended their solo works to be heard, intimately, not from the platform in a large hall. More and more, I have come to realize just how unsatisfactory public performances on a piano are. Even the most exquisite playing comes over weakly, attenuated, and thin. It is all rather like eating a well-cooked dinner with a strong smell of antiseptic in the air.

Emotionally I had had enough now, at any rate on the piano. We got into small talk of no concern. John whispered discreetly in my ear, 'Great stuff, Dicky. This is my phone number, give me a call tomorrow morning.' Then he was away. At last I got a chance to talk to Lena. Her face was animated and responsive now. Odd the way it goes, I thought, mazurkas at eighteen, Beethoven sonatas at twenty-five. I wondered what the trick would be at fifty – aleatoricism? More or less spontaneously we decided to leave. This was a community in which you arrived when you pleased and left when you pleased. It would have suited Alex Hamilton. The hostess – I still didn't know her name – asked me to call up any time I was free. It was all aboveboard and genuine. She kissed me as I left. I thought of poor John on his solitary way back to Pasadena or to wherever he was going. There was nothing like science for the good clean life.

Outside, I took Lena's arm. She said, 'Can I drive you somewhere?'

'Yes, I'm looking for some place to sleep.'

'How am I intended to take that?'

'Quite genuinely. I've got to find a motel.'

'There are plenty.'

She guided the car with a sure hand through the labyrinth of small roads. I was glad I hadn't been left to make my way out at this time of night. It was warm, the car was open, there was a pleasant fragrance in the air. She said, 'I'd like to drive by the sea.'

We parked at the top of a cliff. Below us the sea spread out in a huge luminous phosphorescent arc. I turned to Lena. She smiled at my inquiring look.

I remember very little of where we went, of slipping out of the car into the house, or of the trivia of the bedroom. But I do remember lying there afterwards listening to the roar of the sea. I remember that enough light came through a long window for me to see Lena's face. There were tears standing on her eyelashes. When I brushed them away she smiled. A moment later she was asleep. I lay awake for a little while more, at peace, still listening to the sea, before I too fell asleep.

It was late the following morning when we woke. The house was built very close by the water. The beach was fairly steeply sloping, the sand was good. A few minutes after getting out of bed I was tumbling in the surf. After a quick dry off I padded into the kitchen for breakfast. I had decided I wasn't going to Hawaii, not unless Lena would come too. There seemed no point in my tagging along with the scientists like a camp follower. Over coffee I asked Lena if she had any wish to go out to the islands. 'I'd like to go, but next week I'm working. If you're going to be there for some time I could join you later.' This seemed to be the right compromise.

I rang John during the morning to say I'd prefer not to travel with him the following day but rather come on by myself at the end of the week. There seemed no point in my hanging around in Los Angeles once Lena started at the studios.

The next few days passed all too quickly. We drove around, we swam, and made love and made music. Neither of us had any reason to feel there was anything unique about those days. I was not a soldier going to the wars, someone who might never return. After all, we would meet again in a week or two, if not in Hawaii, in Los Angeles. Yet we parted one morning at the airport with sudden sadness.

The mood lasted with me all the way to the islands. Three hours later I saw them standing up boldly out of a blue sea. I took a taxi from the airport into Honolulu. Soon I was booked into an hotel at Waikiki, close to the sea.

From there I put a call through to John who I knew would be on the island of Hawaii itself. I didn't reach him first shot so I had to leave a message to have him call me back. This forced me to hang around the hotel. When John at last came through, quite a while later, he said it would be best if I made the island hop the following morning. Why didn't I hire a car and take a look around Oahu? I said this was fine by me. It was mid-afternoon by the time I had the car which meant there wasn't a great deal of the day left for sightseeing. I asked at the hotel desk which was the most spectacular beach. The girl suggested I might like to go to the north side of the island to Sunset Beach.

It was warm and sticky as I drove over the twisting mountain road. The beach itself was tremendous, yet somehow I couldn't really get interested. I wondered if this was the way you became old, nothing excited you any more. I drove back by the east coast. After checking my car, I had an early dinner and then went straight to bed. I couldn't sleep. I lay wide awake for an hour, then I got up, dressed, and walked out to the sea.

As I strolled along the flat sand I was in the grip of a fit of loneliness such as I had rarely, if ever, experienced before. It came gradually upon me how much loneliness was increasing in our modern society. I realized it had been a dominating factor in almost all the people I had played to the other night.

I wandered back along the beach wondering whether these ideas, which had a deep validity, I was convinced, could somehow be expressed in sound. Anything new, for it to be worthwhile, must come out of my inner feelings. It couldn't be developed as a mere logical plan. The grandeur of Bach's music came out of his religious impulses, not from his technique. He worked to develop the technique because of the inner convictions, not the other way round.

To the west, away from the city, stars filled the sky. As I looked up to them my senses were suddenly acute and overwhelmingly strong. Reason suggests there could be nothing to it. Yet, knowing now what was to happen, I sometimes wonder whether the future at that moment did not touch me like a cold wind across the face.

5 Allegro Assai

The mood was gone the following morning. The trip from Honolulu to the big island of Hawaii was, I suppose, about one hundred and fifty miles. I was met at Waimea by a car. The country hereabouts was surprisingly flat, considering the four-teen-thousand-foot high Mauna Kea was only some fifteen miles to the south. The journey to the field-station was a short one and soon I was dumping my bags into a room in the sleeping quarters. Although the buildings had a prefabricated look about them they were, nevertheless, very well appointed inside. I had barely finished unpacking when John arrived.

'Just in time,' he said. 'We're beginning to get results. It's already clear the signal is genuinely modulated.'

'You mean the beam really is being used for conveying in-formation?'

'That's what it looks like.'

About midday a party of five army and navy officers arrived. Over lunch everybody started to talk. For a while it was all much the things I knew already, apart from some technical interpolations which didn't interest me. John explained his ideas. Clementi quickly went over the general experimental set-up. The officers got the drift, more or less as I did. They asked questions about the interference fringes, questions I was too shy to ask. Clementi drew a series of loops, by way of answer, looking somewhat like a bunch of bananas. There was a lot of talk about near-fields and far-fields but this was beyond me.

The essential idea seemed to be one of phase. If you have something that oscillates up and down the precise position where it happens to be at a given moment is the phase. What it came down to was this: if you chose a particular moment of time, and then considered the phases over a very big area, they all had to be the same, in order to explain the observations. When he was asked how big the area had to be, John replied:

'According to my calculations about ten times the radius of the Sun.'

'But how can you get a phase correlation over such an enormous area?'

'That's what we all want to know,' muttered Clementi.

The big man padded around and stated sententiously, 'Control phase, and you control the universe.'

'But that's what we do with our radar, isn't it?' asked an elderly, blue-eyed naval officer.

John nodded. 'That's exactly the right way to put it. It's just as if there was a big antenna, measuring ten times the radius of the Sun. Apparently it's beaming a message out into space.'

There was silence for a while.

'What would be the directivity, with an antenna as large as that?' asked another of the officers.

'At a big distance, quite fantastic. The beam would go out into space as an extremely fine pencil.'

Someone had a bright idea.

'What's the chance of our being in the direct beam?'

'Remembering that we are in the near-field, it works out at somewhere between one in ten and one in a hundred, provided the beam is directed more or less along the ecliptic. Less than that if it's directed at random.'

'Isn't it a bit surprising that we just happen to lie in it?'

'We're not necessarily lying in the main lobe. I've thought quite a lot about this point. From a climatic point of view, I mean.'

John had their attention now.

'There must be something like a ten per cent difference in the solar radiation according to whether we're in the main beam or not. Of course we can't know anything directly about this infra-red stuff down here on the surface of the Earth. The infra-red never gets through the atmosphere. But it would have the effect of increasing the boundary temperature of the Earth.'

'By how much?'

'Anything up to ten degrees I would say. What I've been wondering is whether all the mysterious climatic fluctuations the Earth seems to suffer – the ice-ages for instance – could be caused by our relation to this beam. You know, it may not always point in the same direction. Sometimes the Earth could pass through it, during the year I mean. At other times we might miss it entirely.'

Clementi made a kind of humming sound. He wasn't winking. 'A few degrees up, or a few degrees down, is really all that might be needed to make quite big changes of climate. It could be at that. But look here, John, old chap, old fellow, old scoundrel more like, are you hinting that this deal up there might have been going on for thousands of years?'

'I should have thought it extremely likely. If it was something that had just started up right now, well, wouldn't it be ridiculously improbable?'

'Yeah, I suppose so.'

Several of the men were pacing like caged beasts up and down the lounge floor.

There was a silence which everybody seemed reluctant to break. At last, the naval officer with the blue eyes spoke:

'Gentlemen, it's time we came to the real issues. I don't know whether my colleagues and I can be described as having anything more than a watching brief here. But the questions that stand out in my mind are, first, how's it being done, second, what's it for? I must admit I'm personally in a smoke screen but maybe Dr Sinclair has something he'd like to add.'

This was quite a formal speech. I wondered how John would react to it. He shrugged his shoulders and began:

'I think anybody's guesses are as good as anybody else's at this stage. For myself I can't remotely conceive how this phasing trick is being worked. But being worked it surely is, so for the moment we'd better accept that, and go on from there – if we can. We've tested the deduction that the beam is being used to convey information.'

'What information? What the hell is there to send, where and to whom?'

One of the army officers grinned and suggested, 'Maybe it's a TV relay.'

Most of them laughed at this. I noticed John didn't. When the laughter had died down he simply said, 'Could be.' Everybody looked at him, so he went on:

'It may sound crazy but what else can it be? Oh, I don't mean a TV relay strictly. Think of the colossal amount of information that's probably being sent out, of the order of a hundred million bits a second. In a year, that's several thousand trillion bits. Something like a hundred million textbooks a year. What sort of traffic would you need to fill a channel like that?'

'You mean there'd be no point in sending out such a lot of stuff unless there was really something to send?' Everybody laughed at this.

After a further short pause John went on:

'There are two speculative possibilities. This might be an interstellar, or even an intergalactic, relay station. Granted the enormous directionality of the system, the fineness of the pencil beam, these signals could be received at an enormous distance away from us.'

Clementi had obviously been thinking along the same lines. 'The details really aren't as fantastic as the thing itself. But as John says, we know the thing exists, so there's no getting away from it. It's easy enough to do an intensity calculation. If this really is a relay station, if some guy at the other end has even a moderately sensitive detecting device, say only a millionth part as sensitive as our big radio telescopes – as this thing out on the hillside here – then these signals can be picked up – where? Come on, freshman physics! Not just in our own galaxy, but anywhere, out and beyond anything we can see with the biggest telescopes.'

'You mean this is just about the most...' The naval officer broke off whatever it was he was going to say. It was clear to him, as to me, that the wonders of science had gone beyond all reasonable bounds.

I was back in my room that night, jotting down one or two musical ideas, when John tapped on my door. 'Would you like to go for a stroll?'

We slipped out of a side door.

'I don't want any of the others to join us just for the moment.'

We had walked along for two or three hundred yards before he came to the point:

'I've been thinking it would be a good idea if you were to write everything down. I mean from the beginning. I think it would be a good idea to have an account from an unbiased person.'

'You mean a non-scientist?'

'If you like to put it that way, yes.'

My story is built from notes as I made them following this incident. Unfortunately my diary wasn't remotely detailed enough as it has turned out. So perforce I have often had to fill in as best I can from memory – this will explain how it comes about that sharp accounts of what took place are sometimes juxtaposed with obvious lapses of memory – my failure to recollect odd names for instance.

I began to see now why John had more or less press-ganged me into coming along with him. I also felt freer to ask questions with a clear conscience.

'It's all very well to avoid the problem of how this incredible thing is being done but do you have any idea at all about what's really happening?'

We walked on for a little way.

'Not with any precision. The obvious inference is that someone is doing it. I suppose the most straightforward explanation would be to say that it's some creature, some intelligence, on one of the other planets.'

'A major boost to the space programme – eh?'

'As you say, a major boost to the space programme.'

I guessed that John really didn't believe this. When I asked him point blank he replied:

'It's an outrageous explanation fitted to a fantastic situation. Yet anything else seems worse. It's all a question of the way you look at it. When something really new happens most scientists take the line of least resistance. They accept the explanation that involves the least change from their preconceived notions. Which is what I'm doing now.'

'But you don't believe it?' I pressed.

'With me, believing or not believing a particular explanation is more a matter of method than of emotion. If I were emotional I'd be almost certain to plump for what I've just told you. The way I always work is like this. If I find things turning out much as I expect then I follow the line of least resistance, exactly the same as everyone else. But if I find my deductions going wildly wrong it's my instinct to explain my shortcomings by saying that I just haven't got hold of the right idea at all. I don't try to do a patchwork job, to choose the explanation that requires the least possible change from my previous position. I throw the net wide, just as wide as I can.'

By now my eyes were accommodated to the dark. We were able to pick our way across the open grassland with more precision.

'I suppose it's really not fair to twist your arm any further but what does this wide net look like? My own imagination just boggles at the idea of there being something still more strange and unusual than creatures on another planet.'

'I've got nothing definite to go on, except the day on the moor after we came off Mickle Fell.'

'You still think that amnesia business might have had something to do with it?'

'I don't know. What I do know, is that every explanation I can conceive of for that gap of thirteen hours, and for the mark that used to be on my back, is much more weird than this planet business. It suggests to my mind there's a real danger of our concepts going wildly astray.'

'In what sense?'

'Consider the usual science-fiction story. Let me anatomize the situation for you. Science-fiction is a medium that concerns, above all else, life forms other than ourselves. The real life forms of our own planet belong of course to natural history, to zoology, so science-fiction purports to deal with life forms of the imagination. Yet what do we find when we read science-fiction? Nothing really but human beings. The brains of a creature of science-fiction are essentially human. You put such a brain inside a big lizard, and bang-wallop, you have a science-fiction story. Or if you can't be bothered with the lizard-like aspect of the story, you simply put the human brain in a human creature, and call it a humanoid. To make the story go, the humanoid is usually set up as more intelligent than ourselves, with a better technology. Then the story turns on how the dear old magnificent human species manages to deal with the alien threat. It boils down to a new version of indians and cowboys.

'Let me be a bit more serious. If these rather simple-minded notions stopped at science-fiction it wouldn't be so bad. But as soon as we try to think quite seriously about intelligence outside the Earth that's exactly the way our concepts go.'

'So when you talked about a creature on one of the other planets you were really inventing a science-fiction story?'

'That's the way it seems to me.'

'Yet what else could there be?'

'Very hard to say, isn't it? If your brain doesn't have the right concepts you can't really force it to develop them. I'm quite willing to agree there may be lots of creatures more or less similar to us distributed up and down the universe, or even among the stars up there. What I doubt is whether there are any such creatures on Mars or Venus. Even if there were, I don't think they could perform this trick with the Sun.'

'You think it's too big? The Sun I mean. That a creature stuck down on a planet could hardly do anything to a star?'

'I'm more or less sure of it.'

After a short pause, John went off on a new tack. 'In physics, we accept a lot of mysterious things.'

'Such as what?'

'Well, it's very mysterious that our consciousness enables us to take decisions which turn out to improve our description of the world – in circumstances, mark you, when improvement ought to be impossible according to our basic physics.'

'Sounds the sort of thing our religious friends would be glad to hear.'

'They can read it in any textbook if they like. Let me give an example. You take a number of radioactive nuclei of a particular kind, the number being chosen so that there's an even chance of one of them going off in a certain period of time, say ten seconds. Then for ten seconds you surround them with counters, or any other detecting device you might like to use. At the end of the time the question is, has one of them decayed or not. To decide this you take a look at your counters. The conventional notion is that the state of the counters decides whether a nucleus has gone off or not.'

'What you're saying is that if you did this experiment a lot of times your calculations require that in a half of the cases a nucleus will have decayed and in the other half there will have been no decay?'

'Right. But my problem now concerns an individual case. Has there been a decay or hasn't there? How do you decide?'

'I would suppose by looking, which is what you said a moment ago.'

'Of course. But here comes the rub. It is perfectly possible to put your counters, or your bubble chamber, your camera, all your gobbledegook in fact, into your calculations – and we know quite definitely that any attempt to get a definite answer out of calculation will prove completely fruitless. The thing that gives the answer isn't the camera or the counter, it's the actual operation of looking yourself at your equipment. It seems that only when we ourselves take a subjective decision can we improve our description of the world, over and above the uncertainty of our theories. I'm talking about quantum theories now.'

'So you've got a real contradiction?'

I waited as John paused again. He lifted his hand in a gesture. 'There's one possible loophole. We could be wrong in comparing ourselves as physical systems with a camera or a counter or anything like that. The essential thing about a camera is that it's local. Its operation can be described by a strictly finite number of variables, its activities are restricted to a limited volume of space-time. It could be that when we make subjective judgements we're using connexions that are non-local. If this is right the logical ramifications are enormous. It means we can have connexions ranging all over the universe.'

'What's the relation to this business?'

'This affair could have nothing at all to do with our own local planets. It could be on a vastly bigger scale. It needn't have anything to do with human brains in lizard heads.'

'You've one or two fairly definite ideas?'

From long experience I knew that John would not have got himself into this conversation unless there was more than general guesswork behind it.

'There's one thing. You remember we talked about the purpose of this phased infra-red stuff. For God's sake don't tell anyone I don't really go along with that relay station idea. There's another more remarkable possibility. I've got a feeling the more remarkable possibility has a better chance of being right. Think of the enormous volume of communication that must be involved here, the incredibly detailed information. What kind of thing do we know about that would need such a capacity? This is the question I keep asking myself. What was it, a hundred million major textbooks a year? The sort of physics we study needs nothing like that. If you know how, you can put all our basic physics into one book. I suppose you could put most aspects of our technology into a hundred books. The only things I can see around me needing anything like this volume of information are biological organisms, our brain processes for instance, or the information needed to construct a human being.'

The following day I went for a drive round the island. I

went to Volcano House and took a look at the active Kilauea crater. I saw sugar plantations, pineapple fields, rain forests, the sea and the mountains. When I got back to the experimental station I found the place in a wild panic. Somebody told me war had started and that Los Angeles had been destroyed.

6 Agitato

The personal crowded out the general. My first thought was of Lena. I was dry in the throat. I began rushing around with the others, in the hope of finding John or one of his friends. I couldn't really believe the news was true but it didn't need to be true to be frightening. Of course I knew there was a bad situation in south-eastern Asia. Yet I hadn't remotely credited it could blow up into a major war, if that was what this really was. Then I remembered war always seems to come as a surprise to civilians, at any rate it had in 1914. At last I ran into Art Clementi.

'Is there any truth . . .' I began.

'Can't say yet. But something serious seems to have happened. A few of us are going over to Pearl City. We can probably manage to tuck you in if you want to come along. John's going, the Brass want him down there.'

I packed my things as quickly as I could. In a sense, rushing over to Pearl City was a form of panic, a desire to do something, to avoid sitting still and waiting. That's the way terror got you, you just ran aimlessly around in any direction.

It was only when I walked with my bag out to the car park that I found John. I was glad to see he didn't look too worried.

'I find this very difficult to believe. Something's happened all right but it must have become exaggerated. We'd better go over and find out exactly what it is.'

Scarcely a word was spoken on the journey to Hailo airport. Nobody said very much there either. We all got on to the plane in silence. It put down for a short stop in the island of Maui and then went on to Honolulu. A big station wagon was waiting for us. There was very little traffic on the road as we made our way to the naval base. Then came a hold-up when it was found that neither John nor I was an American citizen. After a delay, in which I suppose a number of phone calls were put through, we were separated from the others and told that a car would be made available to take us to a downtown hotel. After the best part of an hour a car did appear and we made away in it. In the car John said, 'I told Art we would go to the Waikiki.'

We got rooms at the hotel. I tried to ring Los Angeles but found all lines engaged. Then I lay flat out on my bed in a quite blank state of mind. I had a call from John on the house phone at about six o'clock suggesting we meet downstairs in the bar for a drink. It seemed as good an idea as anything else. After the drink we went to dinner in the hotel restaurant.

'I wonder if I could have a talk with you chaps?' The speaker was an Australian. We told him to pull up a chair. Clearly he had finished dinner. We were only half-way through the main course. We introduced ourselves, and took stock of our new acquaintance. It struck me I had become far more suspicious, far less free and easy, in the last few hours. I felt as if I was on some kind of an assignment. The Australian had an athletic look about him. His manner was pleasant and open.

'I heard you talking and realized you were a couple of Britishers.'

The clans were certainly drawing together. Our exclusion at Pearl City and now this.

'How about a walk on the beach when you've finished? I'll be in the bar.'

Then he was gone.

Not long afterwards Art Clementi appeared. We naturally wanted to know the news:

'It looks bad, real bad. There's no doubt the west coast has been attacked.'

We tried to get more out of him but either he knew nothing more or he wouldn't say. It was all very odd. It was also odd that Clementi went off without eating dinner with us. He excused himself by saying he had already eaten but I knew from the way he looked at the food that this couldn't be so. What the hell did it mean, the contrast between this frigidity and the uproarious welcome we had received only the other day in California?

We got the beginnings of an answer from our Australian acquaintance. He waited until we were well away on the beach before he would talk. The man was a QANTAS pilot. He had been on a regular flight from Honolulu to the United States.

As he approached the international airport at Los Angeles a message had come through directing him to return.

'There was something crook about it.'

'In what way?'

'It didn't look right. In fact it was all wrong, just as wrong as it bloody well could be.'

'Things wouldn't look very pretty after a nuclear attack.'

I had told John nothing of Helena Summers. In the poor light I don't suppose they could have seen my distress.

'That's just it. If I could have seen a lot of damage, a lot of smoke, I wouldn't have been surprised.'

'There must have been smoke.'

'Well, there wasn't. It was a clear day. Of course I was nearly fifty miles out to sea. Yet as far as I could tell there was nothing.'

We stopped in astonishment. The surf broke loudly, not far away on our right. We waited for the rippling noise to die away.

'Nothing?'

'Not a bloody thing. I could see the whole Los Angeles basin. And I tell you there wasn't a bloody thing there.'

'I tried to ring Los Angeles this afternoon. They told me all the lines were engaged, so there must be something there.'

'Do you think they'd tell you if there wasn't?'

'Didn't you get any signals from the control tower?'

'Not a damn thing. Not a peep. I thought the radio must be out of action. We couldn't pick up anything, not from San Francisco either, or from the control stations to the east. I told the wireless operator to keep trying. He did a big search over the whole shortwave band. Do you know what he came up with?'

'If the war's really started all long-range stuff will be off the air. Local TV stations and news stations will be on, probably.'

'Well, I'll tell you this. I got the control back here, exactly as usual. And I got some shortwave stuff from Britain. And that was it, nothing anywhere else.'

'You got the usual British channels?'

'As far as I could tell. We're a long way off here. So I only got odd snatches. As far as we could judge it was about what was to be expected in a normal way.'

We walked on for a while before John said, 'Could that be

54

the trouble do you think? It seems incredible but if Britain's really on the air in any normal way she hasn't been attacked.'

'It could be.'

'Did you get anything from the west, the other way?'

'From Fiji, nothing from Sydney.'

It didn't make sense, except perhaps for one ray of light.

'Do you think they imagine we've gone neutral? If Britain is more or less normally on the air that's what it looks like.'

'I'd thought of that,' answered John. 'It would fit. If they think we've ratted on them it would be natural enough for them to treat us pretty distantly. Yet it seems fantastic. British policy and American policy are in it together. I would have thought we couldn't keep out even if we wanted to.'

We headed back to the hotel. I asked, 'What are you going to do? With your plane? Go back to Australia?'

The pilot paused for a moment. 'I've given quite a bit of thought to that. I'm supposed to be on a through flight Los Angeles to London, with a refuelling stop in Canada. I suppose if I insist they'll let me take off as long as I agree to keep over Canadian territory all the way.'

'Isn't that the natural thing to do?'

'I suppose so. But I'm leery about it. I can't say exactly why, but I'd prefer it if I could go right through in one hop.'

'I thought the new planes could pretty well do that, at any rate from California. Can't you make it with a light load?'

'I've got one of the old jobs.'

'Pity, because we ought to be getting back home – at any rate if the atmosphere doesn't get warmer around here.'

'Day after tomorrow we have a long-distance plane coming through. It could make the trip. I'll have a word with the captain if you like.'

We said we thought it might be a good idea.

By now we were nearing the hotel. After a drink at the bar I decided to turn in. Sick at heart I took one last look out over the sea before I climbed into bed. Unpleasant emotions seemed inseparable from this damned place. I lay there thinking about Lena. I could remember the tears and the smile which followed them.

What the devil did the Australian mean by saying there was nothing? Not even the dead and the dying? I little realized that I had become separated from Helena Summers by much more than death.

I was wakened the following morning by the phone burring in my ears. It was John saying he was going out to Pearl City, that the climate seemed to have changed back just as suddenly as it had shifted yesterday. I asked him why, but he didn't know. When I came down to breakfast in the coffee shop I found the blue-eyed naval officer waiting for me. We sat down together. I ordered a stack of wheatcakes and coffee. He ordered coffee.

'I'm afraid we owe you a very sincere apology. Yesterday we didn't know where we were, not that we're much better today. But we can see things a bit more clearly now.'

Then he went on to tell me, rather haltingly, much the same as John had already guessed, that radio communications from Britain, apparently still covering the normal radio waveband, had convinced them Britain had somehow managed to stay out of the war. This had made for a peculiar situation so far as we were concerned. They had thought the best thing was to do nothing and say nothing. I said both John and I had appreciated what the situation must look like and we quite understood his position. He became less embarrassed but no less worried. I told him I had a close friend in Los Angeles and could he tell me anything of what had happened there. He looked about him, to see whether anybody was listening, and then said, 'We can't understand it, we just can't understand it. We've sent planes over and – well, there's nothing there, nothing at all.'

I asked if this could be some strange new development in war technique. Yet even as I asked the question I realized it was absurd. The officer shook his head. He looked tired and old and I could see the situation was quite beyond him.

'It may sound horrible. If it had been war, the kind we expected, I would at least have understood what was going on. It looks like a nightmare, as if we were all dreaming. I keep hoping I'll waken up. That sounds kinda silly.'

'Don't you think we ought to stop trying to understand it, at any rate for the time being. Perhaps we ought to get back to the way we were when we were kids. We all took the world the way we found it. Only later as we grew up did we try to make sense of it.'

'Yes, I suppose so. But at my time of life it isn't easy to learn new tricks. You get set in your ways as the years roll past. You see I had a son and daughter-in-law and two kids in Los Angeles.'

We shook hands sadly and he left.

For the next two days I sat in my room writing as hard as I could go. I wanted to get all the old, more normal, stuff down before my standards of judgement became distorted by this strange new world. I knew John and his colleagues would seek me out as soon as the next move was decided. As I say, I was given two days' grace. I emerged from my room only for meals. My fingers grew stiff with writing, always writing, twelve hours a day.

John appeared at last late on the second day. He had not eaten at lunchtime so I went with him back to the restaurant, although I had already had dinner. I asked for the news.

'Fragmentary in the extreme. The balance of opinion still favours war of some sort. Nobody can fit the facts together. It seems quite certain that Los Angeles really has ceased to exist. We don't know much about the rest of the States. In Britain it seems to be just as normal as it is here. There's some activity in Europe, although it doesn't look normal there either. From Russia there's as big a blackout as there is from the American mainland.'

I waited. It was an old trick with John, the dramatic pause.

'Back home they're in just the same mess. We managed to get a message through. They wanted news, saying they're just as much in the dark as we are.'

'I had the old naval chap in again this morning. He doesn't like it at all.'

'The devil is that everything is so normal here. It's only the outside communications that are crazy.'

'Could it be some sort of hoax, some ridiculous psychological experiment, connected with the military programme? To determine the population reaction.'

'Well, if it is, we shall soon know. You remember the Australian. He told us a plane was coming in from Fiji, one that might manage to get through to Britain in one hop? It's here now, it came in yesterday evening, and it's the only real long-range plane in the islands. So they've decided to send it over the States. It can get to somewhere in the region of

Denver or Chicago and still manage to get back here to the islands. The military people have commandeered it. After a bit of argument I've got the two of us included on the trip. I've given them the idea I might come up with some explanation of what's going on.' John ran his hand through his hair and added, 'Some hopes.'

At breakfast the following morning I realized a strange thing had happened in the preceding days, the days in which I had been shut away in my room. From the beginning, from the moment the war rumours first spread, smiles had disappeared, there had been less talk, less laughter, fewer vehicles on the street. Now there was an almost complete silence. Everybody spoke quietly, as if someone or something was listening to what was being said. In these islands of sunshine it was weird and unnerving.

We got to the airport at about nine o'clock. I would say about forty persons, mostly service officers, were already assembled there. I looked around for Art Clementi, hoping to straighten out the misunderstanding and embarrassment of our last meeting, but he wasn't there.

'Looks as though we're taking a very light load,' I said.

'To give as big a range as possible.'

A few minutes later we climbed up an old-fashioned ramp into the rear door of the plane. An Australian girl smiled at us as we enplaned. A few minutes later we were in the air.

We settled down in our seats. The hostess brought us quite large glasses of fresh orange juice. It was a welcome change from the inevitable coffee.

'Australian idea,' said John. 'Genuine stuff, not artificial muck.'

'What's been going on the last two days?'

'I got involved in two things. Damn queer, both of them. I was out at the university, at the seismic department. On the face of it not very exciting. Simple equipment and so on. I'm not familiar with the details of that business so I had to accept what they told me.'

'And what the devil did they tell you?'

'Well, the general background of seismic disturbances – you know there are always slight earth movements going on all the time – has gone up enormously in the last four days.'

'I didn't notice any earthquake.'

58

'Oh, this was below the subjective threshold. But it was much above the usual noise level by several orders of magnitude.'

'Maybe there's been a big earthquake somewhere, a long way off.'

'It couldn't be just one earthquake, it wouldn't last long enough. More like a succession of them. And even that doesn't fit the pattern properly. From a single earthquake, particularly a big one, you get a pretty clean-cut record. This stuff is all confused, it looked like real random noise.'

'What could be doing it?'

'Nobody has the slightest idea. It isn't very dramatic, not like the other things, but I thought I'd mention it. Often it's the non-spectacular things that lead you in the right direction.'

'You said there was something else, two things you'd been looking at.'

'Right. Signals from the rocket have stopped. Art Clementi's boys are getting a blank record.'

'How long did you expect to go on getting a signal before the rocket got too far away from the Earth?'

'Oh, for several weeks more. The natural interpretation is that a small meteorite has hit something in the electronics. It was a rush job so we couldn't take every precaution we would have liked to have done. Yet it's queer to find the signals stopping only a few minutes before the war was announced.'

Several officers and the pilot came to talk to John during the flight. It struck me as odd how much status depends on the social situation. War had reduced us to persons of no account. The present situation, with all its weird implications, taking one as far as the shifting frontiers of science or even beyond that, made John a commanding figure. He was the most distinguished scientist available for consultation. On his coat tails, almost literally, I managed to get into the cockpit as the plane approached the American mainland.

There were a lot of us jammed in there. Yet I could see a great deal more than was possible from an ordinary passenger seat. I gathered it was the Los Angeles basin ahead. The air was completely clear. There was nothing of the banks of brown smog I had seen when we came in from New York two weeks ago. Was it only two weeks ago? It needed no more than the most casual glance to see there was no city here.

'Take a look along the Sierra Madre. Look for the Observatory.'

We were coming lower now, to an altitude of about ten thousand feet I guessed. There were mountains below us, heavily wooded. I noticed there were no fire-rides. We flew immediately above their crests, sharp and jagged. The trees covered the very topmost point. If this was Mount Wilson, there was no observatory here. We left the mountains and came back to the flatter land by the coast, dropping down still further, to only a few thousand feet. It was then we caught brief glimpses of habitation in the woods. The woods were now covering places where only two weeks before there had been great sprawling boulevards, streaming with traffic, swarming with humanity.

But there were signs of life below us and this lifted our spirits to an astonishing degree. The trouble was we couldn't land the plane. An enormous runway was needed for that and no such thing as a runway was to be seen in the wilderness below us. We came low enough to notice a few cultivated patches of land and this was all. Whoever was down there was keeping out of sight.

The itch to get to the ground was overwhelming, I think, to everybody on the plane. Since we had plenty of fuel we did the obvious thing of heading east, into the American mainland. Sooner or later we all felt it must be possible to find an airstrip. Two weeks ago every town of any appreciable size had its airport, with runways extended for the new jets. The day was so clear that even after we climbed back to forty thousand feet we could still see the ground below quite well.

As we flew on we all kept a sharp lookout for towns and roads. We saw neither in the usual sense. There was an occasional rough track through the mountains. Now and again we thought there were further signs of primitive inhabitations. Whether or not there were houses we couldn't say. Further east, and ever further, we went. The search for a place to land was becoming fruitless. We tried Phoenix, or what used to be Phoenix, then Albuquerque, then at last we were over the central plains. We came down very low over Denver. It wasn't entirely easy to be sure we had located the correct place. There were no radio beacons to guide us. All navigation had to be done with the compasses, and even by the old-fashioned method of simply looking down on to the ground. Denver was a good place to look for. The big sudden rise of the Rockies lies only thirty miles or so to the west. That landmark was quite unmistakable, so all we had to do was to fly on a north–south line until the crew felt convinced they had found the right place. Once again we came low, to a thousand feet or so. Below us there were open grasslands. There were no signs of growing crops. Manifestly, the vegetation was in a natural state, a natural ecology.

With the present light load the plane was expected to have a range of between eight and nine thousand miles. So far, we had done about three thousand. Perhaps it would have been wise to have turned back. Yet the desire to find a landing spot was so strong in all of us that we felt impelled to make one more try, in the direction of Chicago. We wouldn't have a great deal to spare in the matter of range, but by taking a more direct route back to Hawaii the pilot thought he would be all right.

We picked up a powerful tail wind. Quite strong radio signals were coming in now from the east, probably of European origin. We found nothing at Chicago, except endless lakes and woods. Then came the critical discussion, to go on or to go back. The big advantage of going back was we knew exactly where we were going. The disadvantage was that we didn't have a great deal in hand in the way of range. We would have to fight the head wind, although this wouldn't matter too much as long as we found a reasonably direct route. The advantage of going on was that radio-guidance systems seemed to be working more or less normally somewhere to the east. And we still had the tail wind so range would be no problem that way. Besides it was manifestly desirable to establish actual physical communication with whatever it was that lay to the east.

Truth to tell, I think everybody wanted to take a look at New York. It was much the same story as we flew over the Appalachians in the fading light. But there were far more signs of life here, far more primitive shacks, it seemed. It all looked as America might have looked around the year 1800. Darkness came on. We saw little more, except twice there were flickering lights below us, fairly obviously camp fires. Then we were out over the Atlantic.

By now we were back in our seats. The stewardess served us with a meal. There wasn't much conversation, and what there was of it was pretty terse. John and I sat silently, each immersed deeply in his own thoughts. The irrational feeling swept over me that somehow the plane had become a world closed in on itself, that it would go on and on flying for ever. We had frequent reports from the pilot, however, to say that radio communication ahead was entirely normal. But perhaps this was just another monstrous deception? Emotionally, I felt we must go on and on until at last we came to our starting point, back in Hawaii; that we would find everything wiped clean even on the islands, just as it was on the American mainland.

I saw John looking repeatedly at his watch. Like me, like all of us, he was finding the passage of time excruciatingly slow. We had still three hours more to go before the next stage in the drama would unfold itself.

In retrospect I am not sure whether the innocence of my mind was an advantage or not. To build any rational explanation of what had happened, of what I had seen, was utterly beyond me. So I was left only with monstrous images and grotesque explanations.

After an age, in which every ten minutes seemed stretched to an hour, as it does in childhood, the little speakers above our heads crackled. The pilot's voice came over to say we had just passed the west coast of Ireland, that we would be landing at London airport in about three-quarters of an hour. Even the harshness of the speakers failed to conceal the relief, the emotional tones, in his voice.

All the evidence was that London airport was working normally. From the tilt of the fuselage you could see we were coming down now. The moon was shining on banks of clouds below us. Then we were down to the clouds and into them. These were the clouds that hang so frequently over the British Isles, blotting out the sun, giving the grey skies I knew so well. The clouds were astonishingly thin, the layer couldn't have been thicker than a few hundred feet. We broke suddenly below it. There on the ground was a multitude of lights. The sheer normality of it, the roads we could now pick out, set up a sharp reaction. I returned quickly to my seat and lay back feeling I might be sick. It wasn't air-sickness, rather that of faintness. Then I saw we were going down to the ground at last. The landing wasn't a good one, there was a big bump as the wheels hit, but at least we were down. Within a few seconds I felt all right again.

As we taxied along the runway I had the odd thought that maybe I had been dreaming. Perhaps I had snoozed away the whole of a perfectly normal flight. It was hard to believe otherwise as the pilot manoeuvred the plane into its final resting spot.

There was an unconscionably long delay before steps appeared and the rear door was opened. We stood up, collected our belongings, and waited in the aisle in precisely the usual fashion. The people ahead began to move slowly. A minute later I was in the open air. We were shepherded by a girl into a waiting bus. There was another delay and then the crew joined us.

I expected to be taken to the usual assembly hall, or waiting hall, or whatever they called it, prior to immigration and customs. But the bus came to a gate that led off the airfield. The gate was opened. While we were halted two policemen got in. Away over on my right, in the distance, I had the impression of an airport crowded with thousands on thousands of people. It was as if they were waiting there, in the hope of seeing planes coming in to land. Soon we were at a traffic light that led out on to the highway. Then we were speeding into London. Here too, as in Honolulu, there was very little traffic. It was a fair guess that we had been brought this way to avoid the crowds, perhaps to avoid reporters and television cameras. Quite evidently, I had not been dreaming.

7 Adagio

We were taken to what was obviously the headquarters of
some intelligence unit. Men in uniform, men in civilian clothes,
were walking around in a strained, taut way. The American
officers were quickly separated from the rest of us. In fact only
John and myself and the Australian crew were in civvies. We
were shown into rough sleeping quarters. John took this without comment. With a grin he said to me, 'They'll soon change
their tune.'

The following morning, after an unappetizing breakfast, two
officers came looking for John. They asked him to follow
them, or more politely to go with them. John insisted I should
go along too. They were doubtful, but once he had told them I
knew as much about the business as he did – a gross exag-
geration – they made no further objections. We were taken to
a waiting car. In the front, beside the chauffeur, was a fellow
whom I took to be a plain-clothes officer of some species or
other.

The car headed out into west London. It kept on into the
country for an hour or thereabouts. At last we turned in at the
gates of a pretty flossy place. The house was vaguely familiar.

'Chequers,' grinned John. 'I told you they'd change their
tune.'

We were received courteously by the Prime Minister himself.
There were a number of other guests, quite a mob of them.
The Prime Minister introduced us round. There was the
Foreign Secretary, the Chancellor, the Minister of Defence,
the Chief of Staff, and about half a dozen other high-ranking
service officers. They were drinking sherry. A glass of the stuff
was pressed into our hands.

John explained my presence by saying I had been making a
complete record of everything that had happened. This seemed
to please everybody, as if a record is equivalent to an explanation. I also noticed how easy it is for a scribe to get
himself into even the most intimate conference. It comes I

supposed from the laziness to which all flesh is prey. I also noticed the heavy preponderance of the military. It struck me wryly that whenever the unusual happens the stock of the military always seems to rise.

Before lunch John gave an excellent and precise account of what had happened in California, in Hawaii, and on the flight back across America. His narrative was put together so concisely and with such logical consistency that his audience listened without comment or question until it was finished. Then everybody waited for the Prime Minister to comment:

'Obviously you've been thinking of explanations for all this. You've given us the facts. But what do they mean?'

'It's too early to say, sir. It's common dictum I believe among lawyers that one must wait for all the evidence to be in before forming an opinion. I've been waiting for all the facts. You must have an awful lot of things we don't know anything about.'

'We've got plenty of facts, but I don't mind telling you we haven't the slightest idea what they mean. You've given us a pretty succinct account of the American situation. Here's what's happened to us. As far as we can make out everything is quite normal in Britain. From the American mainland we've had absolutely nothing, which doesn't surprise me in view of what you've just said. From Europe too there's been a blackout except in the last few hours.'

'When did the blackout start?'

'Oh, nearly two days ago.'

'At 10.37 p.m.'

One of the officers had consulted a notebook. I felt there must be something wrong here. John was looking puzzled:

'That's only about thirty-six hours. It happened four days ago with us.'

It was their turn to look surprised.

'You mean you lost contact with the American mainland four days ago?' asked the Chancellor.

We both affirmed that this was so.

'Very strange, very strange.'

The Prime Minister was drumming his fingertips on the table.

John went on, 'That's another interesting fact. You were talking about Europe, what's going on there?'

'We don't know.' This from the Minister of Defence.

'You mean it's just as blank as the American mainland?'

'No, it isn't. We've been getting wireless messages but they're strange in every conceivable respect.'

'Why haven't you sent planes over?' I broke in.

The Prime Minister looked at me for a few seconds. I saw his eyes were dark and troubled. 'Of course we sent planes over. They never returned.'

On this new and sombre note we sat down to lunch. A short menu had been typed. I was engrossed in my own thoughts, hardly listening to the discussion, significant as it might be. Idly I looked at the menu. It was dated September the 19th. Of course it must be a mistake. I waited until there was a lull in the talk and then asked, feeling very foolish, whether the date on the menu was right. The triviality of the question riveted everybody's attention. A few seconds went by in which I had the impression they were all ticking off the days in their minds. Then someone said, 'I think it's right.' Another added, 'Of course it's right.' The Prime Minister looked at me and asked, simply, 'Why?'

'Because according to my reckoning it should be somewhere in the middle of August. I think the 13th, certainly within a day or two of that. What's your reckoning, John?'

'Somewhere about that, within a day or two. I've been so heavily occupied that I've really lost precise contact. Yet there isn't the slightest doubt we're still in August. At least Dick and I are in August.'

At this very dramatic point the girl serving the food whispered something to the Prime Minister. He nodded and she went away. A moment later a young lieutenant in uniform appeared. He went to the Chief of Staff, stood behind his chair as if to serve some dish, saluted, and handed him an envelope. The Chief of Staff turned and said, 'Thank you. You can wait outside.'

Everybody watched the envelope being slit open very precisely with a knife. I would have ripped it open with thumb and finger myself. We watched the Chief of Staff reading with growing astonishment. Then he got up and took the papers to the Prime Minister. He stood behind the Prime Minister's chair, waiting for them to be read through. Then the Prime Minister said:

'It's jibberish. Here's a sample:

My views are known to you. They have always been 'defensive' in all theatres but the west. But the difficulty is to prove the wisdom of this now that Russia is out. I confess I stick to it more because my instinct prompts me to stick to it, than because of any good argument by which I can support it.

Where the devil did this stuff come from?'
The Chief of Staff handed the Prime Minister another sheet. The Prime Minister went on:
'Apparently a man in uniform approached the Dover dock authorities this morning. He was in a distraught frame of mind. He insisted on being provided with transport to take him to London, to the War Office. Police took him in custody and found this letter on him. That all?'
'That's all I have here.'
'Why the hell should we be bothered by some lunatic? There must be thousands of them around just at the moment.'
This point of view commended itself to me for every crackpot in the country would now be at work. I could see the ranters in Hyde Park predicting the end of the world.
'There's something very familiar about that passage,' said the Minister of Defence in a puzzled voice.
'Yes,' nodded the Chief of Staff, 'and I think I know where it comes from.' He turned to the Prime Minister, 'If you'll excuse me, sir, I'd like to take a look in the library.'
We all followed him to the library. He looked at the shelves, here and there, for a while. Then with a satisfied grunt he pulled out a volume. He flicked through the pages until at last he came to what he wanted.
'Here it is, the exact passage. You can see for yourselves.'
He held the book down on the table. It was indeed there, exactly as I remembered the Prime Minister reading out a few moments before. It was part of a letter, the rest of which I supposed the Prime Minister hadn't bothered with. Then I noticed the volume was an official war history.
'It's part of a letter from Sir Douglas Haig to Sir William Robertson, written 27 September 1917.'
Coffee was served in the library. We sipped it silently until John said:
'I wouldn't take this as a hoax.'

'How would you take it?' asked the Prime Minister.

'That's another matter. What I mean is our natural impulse is to take it as a hoax because that's the way we'd like to see it.'

'You're not suggesting we should take it literally?'

'I think we ought to know more about it. What about the man they got the letter from? You say he was dressed in uniform. What was the uniform? Surely the people in Dover can tell us. And where did he come from? Did he come from the sea? Why not find out before we get into an argument?'

The Chief of Staff went away. He came back half an hour later, his face ashen grey.

'The man was dressed in a sergeant's uniform, exactly as he would be in 1917. He did come from the sea. They found the boat. There were more than a hundred other passengers. They're all dressed in the uniforms of 1917, or rather they were before they were moved *en bloc* to the local mental hospital. Every one of them swears we are in the year 1917.'

John banged his hands together for a few seconds, 'That's what I expected was going to happen. On a small scale it's the only explanation that makes sense. There's one thing I'd like to find out before coming to the point though.'

There was a phone in the library. In a bemused state of mind I heard John's voice – apparently involved in a technical discussion. After the call was finished, he said:

'Yes, there's been a lot of Earth movement here too, not much below subjective threshold. The noise level is much higher than it was in Hawaii. Normally this is one of the quietest parts of the Earth.'

'What do you get out of that?'

'Nothing in itself. But that was the way it had to be for consistency. I think I know now *what* has happened, although I haven't the slightest idea of *how* or *why*. In fact it's pretty obvious, isn't it?'

We were leaning forward in our chairs. John went on:

'I'll put it as crudely as I can. We've got ourselves into some kind of time-machine. Remember the old Wells story?'

The Chancellor smiled wryly, 'You mean about the fellow who invented a black box in which you could travel either forwards or backwards in time?'

'That's right, a remarkable black box it was. But our time-machine is much more singular. It's not just a case of our being precipitated into other moments of time. And I don't think anybody else has been either. I think everybody, all over the Earth, will have the impression they're living quite normally in the present, as they understand the present. Nobody has noticed any sudden shift of time and nobody will do so, except in the way Dick here did while we were at lunch.'

The Prime Minister pulled a face and threw out his arms in a wide gesture, 'Let's try to see through a glass a little less darkly. Is there any reality in the discrepancy of a month, or are you under some hallucination, or are we under an hallucination?'

'Neither. We're both right. There is no inconsistency in it's being 19 September here in Britain, and the year being 1966. And there would have been no inconsistency to us in the time being the middle of August if we had stayed in Hawaii. It was only when we got together that the discrepancy came out.'

This touched them all off into animated comment. The Chancellor's voice stood out above the rest, 'You mean there are different times in different places on the Earth?'

'That's right. That's the way it must be. In Hawaii it is the middle of August 1966, in Britain it is 19 September 1966, on the American mainland I would guess it is somewhere before the year 1750, in France it is the end of September 1917.'

This was enough for the Prime Minister. 'If there's any possibility you're right we've got a lot of things to do, and without delay. I'm going to suggest we meet back here in four hours, shall we say?' There were nods around the room. Without further ado the Chief of Staff got up and went out. He was followed by the other officers. It was clear the Chief of Staff, the Chancellor, and the Minister of Defence, also felt the need for action, so John and I went out into the garden. After pacing around for a while we decided to go for a walk.

'I see everything fits together, that way. But every instinct, every emotion I've got, rebels against it,' I said with some warmth as we strode out along a country lane.

'Because, like all of us in our daily lives, you're stuck with a grotesque and absurd illusion.'

'How's that?'

'The idea of time as an ever-rolling stream. The thing which is supposed to bear all its sons away. There's one thing quite certain in this business: the idea of time as a steady progression from past to future is wrong. I know very well we feel this way about it subjectively. But we're the victims of a confidence trick. If there's one thing we can be sure about in physics it is that all times exist with equal reality. If you consider the motion of the Earth around the Sun, it is a spiral in four dimensional space-time. There's absolutely no question of singling out a special point on the spiral and saying that particular point is the present position of the Earth. Not so far as physics is concerned.'

'But there certainly *is* such a thing as the present. Without the ideas of the past, the present, and the future we could make no sense at all out of life. If you were aware of your whole life at once it would be like playing a sonata simply by pushing down all the notes on the keyboard. The essential thing about a sonata is the notes are played in turn, not all at once.'

'I'm not really trying to say the present is without validity. Rather that it can't have any validity in physics.'

'Then physics isn't everything? A big admission for a physicist, isn't it?'

'Remember the night we were out walking, back in Hawaii? I said then there were parts of our experience which simply defied physical law. I can develop those ideas a lot further. In a way I'd sooner get it off my chest now, rather than later. It sounds too crazy to put before a lot of people. Yet I'm sure something along these lines must be right. I'm going to put it in terms of a parable. Suppose you have a lot of pigeon holes, numbered in sequence, one, two, and so on ... up to thousands and millions, and millions of millions if you like. In fact the sequence can be infinite both ways, if you prefer.'

I said that I didn't mind. John went on, 'All right, let's come now to the contents of the pigeon holes. Suppose you choose one of them, say the 137th. You find in it a story, as you might find one of those little slips of paper in a Christmas cracker. But you also find statements about the stories you'll find in other pigeon holes. You decide to check up on whether these statements about the stories in the other pigeon holes are right or not. To your surprise you find the statements made about earlier pigeon holes, the 136th, the 135th, and so on, are substantially correct. But when you compare with the pigeon holes on the other side, the 138th, the 139th, ... you find things aren't so good. You find a lot of contradictions and discrepancies. This turns out to be the same wherever you happen to look, in every pigeon hole. The statements made about pigeon holes on one side are always pretty good, those made about pigeon holes on the other side are at best diffuse and at worst just plain wrong. Now let's translate this parable into the time problem. We'll call the particular pigeon hole, the one you happen to be examining, the present. The earlier pigeon holes, the ones for which you find substantially correct statements, are what we will call the past. The later pigeon holes, the ones for which there isn't too much in the way of correct statements, we call the future. Let me go on a bit further. What I want to suggest is that the actual world is very much like this. Instead of pigeon holes we talk about states.'

'I understand what you're saying. You have a division into a number of states. Choice of any one of them constitutes the present. My problem is, who decides which pigeon hole to look in, the one that constitutes the present?'

'If I could answer that question I'd be a good half-way towards solving everything. Before I say anything about it let me ask *you* a question. Suppose that in each of these states your own consciousness is included. As soon as a particular state is chosen, as soon as an imaginary office worker takes a look at the contents of a particular pigeon hole, you have the subjective consciousness of a particular moment, of what you call the present. Think of the clerk in an office taking a look, first at the contents of one pigeon hole, then at the contents of another. Suppose he does this, not in sequence, but in any old order. What is the effect on your subjective consciousness? So far as the clerk himself is concerned, he's jumping about all over the place among the pigeon holes. So your consciousness jumps all over the place. But the strange thing is that your subjective impression is quite different. You have the impression of time as an ever-rolling stream.'

We walked on for a while. I saw that if the contents of a pigeon hole could never be modified then John was right. It would be possible for his clerk to look into a particular pigeon hole a dozen times or more and you'd never know about it. All you could be aware of, on his idea, was the contents of a pigeon hole, not when or how it was sampled. But there was one thing that bothered me:

'Doesn't the idea of a sequence of choices on the part of your clerk itself imply the flow of time? If it does, the argument gets you nowhere.'

'I'm sure it does not. A sequence is a logical concept in which time doesn't really enter at all.'

I saw in a general sort of way what he meant. Yet I was troubled. 'But if you have a rule that requires you to pass from one pigeon hole to the next, like passing from one number to the next, isn't it really exactly the same as a smooth flow of time?'

'If the rule were the one you say, yes certainly. But you could have rules that didn't require the next number to be the succeeding pigeon hole. Look, suppose we do it this way. We could choose number 1, then number 100, then number 2, then number 99, and so on until we've had every pigeon hole from 1 to 100. Then we could do the same thing from 101 to 200. That would be a different kind of rule. In fact there are infinitely many ways in which you can lay down rules, if the sequence itself is infinite. Any particular rule establishes what we call a correspondence between the pigeon holes and the choices. If every pigeon hole is chosen exactly once we have what mathematicians call a one-one correspondence. If every pigeon hole is chosen many times we have a one-many correspondence. The crux of my argument is that you get exactly the same subjective experience whatever the correspondence you choose. It doesn't matter what order you take the pigeon holes, it doesn't matter if you choose some or all of them a million times, you'd never know anything different from the simple sequential order. All you can know is the original contents of the pigeon holes themselves.'

'So really the choices could be an incredible hotch-potch. You could have youth and old age interlaced with each other and you'd never know?'

'Not only that, but you could experience your youth a million times over and you'd never know. If the clerk were to put a note in a pigeon hole whenever he used it, then of course you could know you'd had a certain experience before. But as long as he leaves no note you can never know.'

'I suppose so. Where have we got to now?'

'Quite a way. We've got our sequence of pigeon holes, that's the physical world. We don't think of one pigeon hole as having any more significance than another, which agrees with what I said before. We don't think of one particular state of the Earth as having any more significance than any other state of the Earth. We've completely eliminated the bogus idea of a steady flow of time. Our consciousness corresponds to just where the light falls, as it dances about among the pigeon holes. It lights up first one, then another, in some sequence that is quite irrelevant.

'Now let's come to the hard part. What is this light? I'm no longer talking in terms of a clerk in an office, because I don't want to get bogged down in human images. All our pigeon holes are in darkness except where the spot of light falls. What that light consists of, where it comes from, we know nothing. It lies outside our present-day physics.

'You remember I told you that it's possible to defy our own present-day physical laws and still to make a clear gain in our assessment of the world. You remember the radio-active nuclei with the counters surrounding them? We wanted to know whether or not in a certain period of time a nucleus had undergone decay. I said there was only one way to find out. By looking. In other words by using the spot of light in our pigeon hole. My strong hunch is that it's the spot of light that permits decisions which lie outside the laws of physics. This is why I'm so sure something else must be involved. It doesn't need to be anything mystical. It may be subject to precise description, to law and order, the same as in our ordinary physics. It may only be mysterious because we don't understand it.'

'There's certainly a lot of things I don't understand. This light of yours, or whatever you like to call it, how does it decide that you are you and I am me?'

'That could be another illusion. Look, along one wall of our office we have one complete set of pigeon holes, all in their nice tidy sequence. Along another wall we have another set of pigeon holes. Two completely different sets. But there is only one light. It dances about in both sets of pigeon holes. Wherever it happens to be, there is the phenomenon of consciousness. One set of pigeon holes is what you call *you*, the other is what I call *me*. It would be possible to experience both and never know it. It would be possible to follow the little patch of light wherever it went. There could be only one consciousness, although there must certainly be more than one set of pigeon holes.'

I found this a staggering idea. 'If you're right it would be possible to be a million people and never know it.'

'It would be possible to be much more than that. It would be possible to be every creature on every system of planets, throughout the universe. My point is that for every so-called different creature, for every different person, you need a separate set of pigeon holes. But the consciousness could be the same. There could even be completely different universes. Go back to my decaying nucleus. Hook up a bomb which explodes according to whether you have decay of a nucleus or not. Make the bomb so big that it becomes a doomsday machine. Let it be capable – if exploded – of wiping out all life on the Earth. Let the whole thing go for the critical few seconds, you remember we were considering whether a nucleus would decay in a particular ten seconds? Do we all survive or don't we?

'My guess is that inevitably we appear to survive, because there is a division, the world divides into two, into two completely disparate stacks of pigeon holes. In one, a nucleus undergoes decay, explodes the bomb, and wipes us out. But the pigeon holes in that case never contain anything further about life on the Earth. So although those pigeon holes might be activated, there could never be any awareness that an explosion had taken place. In the other block, the Earth would be safe, our lives would continue – to put it in the usual phrase. Whenever the spotlight of consciousness hit those pigeon holes we should be aware of the Earth and we should decide the bomb had not exploded.'

We walked on and on. There were weird implications here.

'You speak about completely different worlds, different universes. Do you think there was a world in which everything went normally? I know I'm not using words perhaps in the way you'd like me to, but I think you can get the idea. Was there a world in which none of these queer things happened?'

'I don't have any doubt about it. There was certainly a world in which, on 27 September, the men in the trenches in Flanders had Lloyd George as their Prime Minister. We know what happened in that world. It remains to be seen what will happen in this one.'

I thought about this for a moment and then burst out, 'You don't mean to say those men out there are going through the same experiences that men actually went through in 1917? All the mud and the shellfire?'

'Yes, of course. We're not in a pretty world.'

'But don't you see what it means? Damn it all I had an uncle killed in those Flanders battles. For all I know he's out there now.'

'For all you know he may not be killed this time. For all you know you may see him. It's fifty years on or thereabouts, so I don't suppose there'll be many queer cases. I mean of men being alive twice.'

Incredulously, I realized what he meant, someone who had survived the trench battles might still be living. There might be two of them, a young man out there in 1917 and an old man here in 1966.

'But it's fantastic. There can't be two of you.'

'You don't seem to take much notice of what I've been talking about. Remember the states of consciousness, remember the subjective impression of consciousness is not the same thing as the pigeon holes of the physical world. The consciousness of the man in the trenches is not the same as the old man living over here. The pigeon holes are different and they can never be lighted up by the same spot of light.'

'You mean the spot could dance about between the two of them but so long as the pigeon holes are different there would be the subjective impression of their being totally different individuals.'

'Exactly the same as you and I have the impression of being different.'

We walked back in silence. I think both of us were overwhelmed, not only by these ideas, but by the situation that was soon to develop.

We got back to the garden. Then an odd detail occurred to me, 'What was all that stuff about seismic disturbances?'

'My idea, only a fancy if you like, runs something like this. I've told you we're living in a new physical situation. A new bunch of pigeon holes. The game, as I see it, is that the new pigeon holes are similar in most respects to some of the pigeon

75

holes in the other system. It's as if the present world were built out of copies of bits of the old world. Do you remember the day on the moor below Mickle Fell? Don't you realize it was a copy that came back to the caravan that night? Not quite a perfect copy, the birthmark was missing.

'Well, this whole world is a copy of some of the bits from another, the more normal world. This world may be queer by every standard we're used to but the bits must have a proper relation to each other.'

'You mean there's nothing supernatural in it?'

'You might put it that way. Well, look what's involved. Think about the Earth. Things change slowly as the years pass. Landforms are not quite the same now, in 1966, as they were in 1866. So if you copy the part of the Earth that corresponds to the England of 1966, and try to fit it to the Europe of 1917, and to the America of 1700 or 1800, things won't exactly match.'

An idea was working itself around in my head. 'You'd need a lot of information, wouldn't you, to make copies like that?'

John paused as we entered the house. 'Right you are, Dicky my boy. A lot of information. Remember what I said about that infra-red transmission. It was taking an awful lot of traffic.'

'Traffic needed for the copying.'

John nodded and added in a whisper, almost as if he were afraid of being overheard, 'Needed for the copying. We still don't know *how* it was done but at least we know *why*. Different worlds remembered and then all put together to form a strange new world. We shall find out more as we go along. This isn't the end of it.'

8   Allegro Molto e con Brio

As soon as we returned to the house John was collared by one of the service officers. I had spotted a piano earlier in the day. I went to see if there was any chance of my being able to play. Luckily the room with the piano was unoccupied so I shut the door and began to run my fingers over the keyboard. I was horribly out of shape and the first few minutes were pretty bad. I can't remember exactly what I played. Fragments here and there mixed in with a lot of improvisation. I was pretty wound up. For me this was the best way to get any tensions out of my system.

I became aware that someone had entered the room. It was the Prime Minister.

'I hope you don't mind my playing a bit. There didn't seem to be anybody about.'

'Not in the least. It's a relief to hear something different from this appalling situation we're in.'

'Is it true then? About Europe I mean?'

'There doesn't seem to be any doubt about it. Evidence is coming in from all directions. By radio, and by ships coming into port. The whole thing's a fantastic chaos. Whenever a ship comes in, both sides, those on board and those on shore, think the other is completely mad.'

'What are you going to do?'

'That's what we're going to decide. We must put an end to it somehow.'

'Sinclair thinks the situation is real. So far as the soldiers in France are concerned it's real, nothing different from what it was.'

'I don't know which is the more surprising thing, the facts, the situation, or the whole psychology of my own position. It's all completely changed.'

'I can see everything's changed, but what especially worries you?'

'Well, it's not unlike a rather delightful and remarkable story I once heard. About a wagon train crossing the United States during the last century. Two children happened to survive an Indian attack, their parents and friends being killed. One was a boy of twelve, the other a girl of three. The little boy took on the responsibility of getting his sister to California, and somehow succeeded. A complete change from dependence to responsibility. For the last two decades we've been drifting here in Britain in a thoroughly aimless fashion. There was nothing we could do to have any real effect on the world. After the responsibilities of the nineteenth century we'd suddenly become peripheral. Of course we've been pretending, I've been pretending, that we could have influence in other countries, and so influence the course of events. But it was a pretence really designed to keep up our own self-respect. Now everything's suddenly changed, just as it did for those two children. It seems as if what's happening in Europe, and what's going to happen, depends utterly and completely on us.'

The Prime Minister paced rapidly up and down the room. There was suddenly a decisive air about him, an attitude far removed from the bumbling policies of the last few years.

The number of visitors at Chequers had increased sharply during the afternoon. In addition to the politicians and the military there were now economists and two professors of history from Oxford. Messages from the outside world were constantly arriving, replies were constantly being sent. A buffet supper had been arranged. We took platefuls of food to a long table, sat down, and the discussion began. The Home Secretary said an immediate policy decision must be made, within the hour.

'We've reached the stage where something really definite must be said to the people. It can't be very long before the truth gets known. The strong westerly winds of the last few days have dropped. People in the south, particularly in Kent, can actually hear the gunfire in Flanders.'

The Prime Minister agreed to make an appearance on television, to make a frank statement about the whole position. Messages to the B B C and I T V were instantly dispatched.

Then the meeting got down to the problem in everybody's mind, how to stop the tragedy in France. Not a single person round the table had any thoughts otherwise. At all costs the disastrous attacks of early October, the attacks inevitably leading to the mud of Passchendaele, had to be prevented.

With the superior technology of 1966 it was at first sight easy to force a dictated peace on all the combatants. But how could the deadly weapons of the post-nuclear era be explained to minds still immersed in the second decade of the century? A simple display of force would be almost meaningless. Nor was there any prospect of peace being imposed through conventional weapons. In fact the conventional weapons at the disposal of the Prime Minister and his colleagues were negligible in total weight compared to the weapons possessed by the European armies. Guns and tanks were now vastly more refined, it was true, but their numbers were far too small to have any real effect. Only with planes and bombs could anything be done in this line. The air marshals confidently asserted that with complete mastery of the air it would be possible to destroy railway communications on the German side. In this way it would be possible to cut off all supplies to the German side of the fighting line. It was generally agreed, however, that this would only be done as a last resort, if the Germans were unwilling to take an immediately negotiated peace seriously.

The historians were called in at this point, to assess the German attitude to the war in 1917. There was a lot of talk about German political parties, the Social Democrats, the Centre, about the army and the Junkers. Surprisingly perhaps, the opinion was that negotiation might be easiest with the Junkers. It was said their chief motive in fighting the war, besides maintaining the prestige of the German army, was to hold on to their estates in East Germany. The Social Democrats were apparently wrong in the head, expansionist in outlook, and the Centre was worse than impossible.

The French position was plainly tricky. Their country had been violated, their army was passing through a difficult psychological phase, and their only dream was the eventual defeat of Germany. It was open to question whether the French would take kindly to a negotiated peace. The Prime Minister must visit Paris without delay, it was agreed.

At this point the problem of communication with the continent came in for discussion. It was pointed out that the first planes sent from Britain had failed to return. Perhaps the crew members had been taken for madmen, or perhaps the planes had been shot down? I saw the hint of a smile on John's face and knew he had a different explanation. Later he told me those planes had simply flown into – nothingness, before the different zones of the Earth were fully joined.

The opinion was that there would be no difficulty in landing in France provided a strong force of planes was sent. Then the problem of what to do about the British army came up for discussion. This was a matter of some delicacy. Yet even the Chief of Staff agreed that the commanding officers, particularly Sir Douglas Haig, must be recalled without delay. This would be a matter of difficulty, it was realized. The simplest method might be a letter purporting to come from Lloyd George, which would involve forging the old gaffer's signature. Arrangements were immediately put in hand.

Lastly it was agreed to mount an intense psychological campaign. Scores of heavy transport planes would be sent over the fighting line with thousands of tons of leaflets. There would be leaflets for the British, the French, and the Germans. They would say the same thing, they would tell the common soldier to stop it, not to fire another shot, another shell. This would be on the full authority of the British government.

As I heard these preparations being put in train I wondered to myself what it was that had changed in the British government between 1917 and 1966. Here was the Prime Minister in much the position Lloyd George had been in in 1917. Yet, whereas Lloyd George's thoughts had been wholly on how to prosecute the war more efficiently, we were now discussing it on the basis of an instant ceasefire. Nobody around the table had the slightest doubt of what must be done. I saw the difference came from the condition of our minds. In 1917, 1917 in Britain, nobody had been able to think outside the war situation. No doubt everybody wanted the war to stop. Yet everybody in 1917 had lacked the confidence to take the necessary steps. In 1966 our minds were completely outside that situation.

Everybody now had an inner confidence that the situation could be dealt with, somehow. This confidence, I saw, came from the technology of 1966. If our high-speed planes had been taken away, if there were no nuclear weapons in the background, if our industries were not enormously more efficient than the European ones, then we might have found ourselves thinking differently. Our escape from the mentality of 1917 really came from a lack of the fear that haunted the British government in 1917.

When the economists began to speak I realized that our situation in the long term wasn't any too favourable, however. Our technology depended to a considerable extent on large imports of oil. These would no longer be forthcoming, if the world of 1917 existed also in the Middle East. Here it transpired that absolutely nothing had come from the armies in the East, nothing from Egypt or from Mesopotamia. It was agreed this should be looked into forthwith. There would have to be a large-scale conversion back to coal as an energy source. And our coal reserves in 1966 were not too good. Above all, where would we get food imports? With the United States and Canada out of the picture, there was no simple answer to this question. Nothing was known yet about Australia. So there was still some hope of food from the Antipodes. But this was only a hope. It was manifest that the only satisfactory policy for the world of the future was to use the manpower of Europe. With the war ended, every available part of Europe must be put to food production. Oil production must be started in the Middle East without further delay.

I wasn't clear where John and I would come into this picture. When the meeting broke up for a short rest, at about nine o'clock, John got me on one side. He told me he had made arrangements, with the Prime Minister's approval, to get a survey of the world started. If it was 1917 in Europe, about 1750 in North America, there was no telling what it was on the rest of the Earth.

We would use one of the big long-distance planes, at any rate in the first instance. We would make a survey for possible landing places. If there were none, then at a later stage we would have to use flying boats, which could quickly be made available for our use. With these we could land on water, more or less as we pleased, provided the weather was fine. All this was clearly an excellent idea and I was not at all disappointed to be in on it. Yet the situation in Europe, its inner psychology, fascinated me. I hoped we would remain fairly close to events as they developed.

The Prime Minister left to make his speech to the nation. Everybody crowded around a television set as the time for the telecast at last came up. It was a good clear account of the situation, gravely delivered. I could not help wondering what the effect would be on the average viewer. Two months ago it would have seemed raving madness. But now the people would be partially prepared for it. I remembered the crowds back at London airport the previous evening. For all I knew, an end to uncertainty would prove more a relief than otherwise.

We also watched the programme which followed the Prime Minister. With their usual pertinacity, the news agencies must already have discovered the truth. A B B C team of commentators had managed to get across to France. Well-known faces appeared. They had lost their usual smooth technical competence. Wild and distraught now, they were with the British army at Ypres.

We learnt that most of their number had been arrested by the army authorities but a film of what they had found there had been smuggled out of France, presumably with the aid of a light aircraft. To me, the First World War has always had the aspect of a nightmare viewed from the comforting light of the day. Here it was displayed in all its nightmare qualities with the urgency of the present about it. The camera spared us neither the mud, nor the shellfire, nor the wounded and the dead. There were interviews with the living, conjuring up visions of hell. Then quite suddenly it was all over. With mature perception, the B B C announced a complete closure of all its services for the night; for nothing in the way of a normal programme could possibly have followed what we had just seen.

The next day there was an outcry from the Press. *The Times* demanded that whatever was going on in France must be stopped, instantly, without delay. The cry was echoed on every hand. It was clear that action must be swift and immediately effective if the government was to survive even for a week. The irony of the change in outlook of the British people over fifty years escaped almost everyone.

For the next month little useful work was done by the population at large. Most people spent a large part of their time within range of a television set. Everybody in any way immediately involved in the crisis itself worked, however, with a furious intensity. The day after our conference at Chequers we were told to proceed on our voyages of exploration. So we were back at London airport, back with our Australian friend and his plane. We took off early on the morning of 21 September, as the date was here in Britain. Our mission was to proceed east, to the battlefront between the German and Russian armies. It occurred to me that the Tsar was still in power in Russia, Lenin and the Bolsheviks had not yet appeared. This would have given great satisfaction to the Americans if they had been there to appreciate it. Of course there was still Hawaii. This was another ironical situation, for the fiftieth state had suddenly become the first.

I wondered whether the pilot would make a deliberate excursion into northern France. I was rather glad he did not. I needed no further convincing about what was going on there. We were soon across the North Sea and over the southern part of Denmark. Then we headed more or less due east. At our height we were quite immune from any primitive anti-aircraft fire. Our immediate objective was Berlin. Although we had no radio guidance, apart from the fixes which we got from stations back in Britain, we found the city without undue difficulty. There, thirty thousand feet below us, was the city of the Kaisers. War stricken now, its people ill-clad and hungry, dreading the approach of winter, the fourth winter of war. Twenty-five years earlier we should have been dropping bombs. Today we dropped some twenty tons of leaflets which had been printed in a high priority rush job the previous day. I was fascinated by the thought of what the people would think when they read:

BRITISH GOVERNMENT DEMANDS CESSATION OF WAR

There followed a precise statement of the numbers of the dead, wounded, and missing. They were given month by month, for the different battlefronts. To the authorities in Germany they would appear quite fantastically accurate, for they had been compiled from the Germans' own post-war records. The leaflets fluttering down through the air below us were likely to prove vastly more effective than a plane load of bombs could ever be. There would also be the fantasy generated by the sight from the ground of our plane, monstrous by the standards of 1917. The shattering effect of all these factors was clear to me.

Clouds gathered as we flew further east. We could see

nothing of what lay below. Our mission was to discover the state of things in Russia, if possible to report on the eastern battlefront. To do this it would be necessary to go down to lower altitudes to break through the cloudbank which now obscured our view. There seemed no particular reason to fear anti-aircraft fire.

We must have been somewhere near the Russian border when the pilot set us on a gentle glide. To begin with it was very much the same as it had been coming into London airport on our flight from Hawaii. There we had come down on to a sea of clouds, had gone quite quickly through it, and had at last come out with a clear view of the ground. It had been exactly what we expected and hoped it would be. Now as we came out through the clouds we saw a great flat plain stretching away in all directions, brown and desolate, without the slightest trace of vegetation. It was a wilderness of bare rock.

We flew on towards the east. An hour later we were somewhere over the position of Moscow. The clouds were clearing. To our astonishment what looked like a vast ocean lay ahead. Yet it was an ocean such as none of us had seen before. As we came clear of the clouds we were dazzled by an intense light from below, coming from the direction of the Sun. The ground was evidently a far better reflector than the waters of the oceans. Compared to the intense light towards the south, the north was dark, a dark purple. Once we had learnt to avoid the southern glare we were amazed by the profusion of colours the sunlight was bringing out in the material below us.

We came down low, to about five hundred feet on the altimeter. Still we could see nothing but a smooth plain. There were no familiar landmarks from which we could judge our height, it all looked the same from any height. There were no trees, houses, no rocks or boulders, nothing.

Still we flew on. Two hours later we were over what should have been the Ural mountains. The level plain was unbroken. There was neither hill nor valley. There was always the iridescent plain below us. We discussed the possibility of landing. There was no problem about finding a flat place, it was all flat. What we didn't know was whether the surface was firm or soft. If it were soft we should simply bog in. Take-off would be impossible even if the pilot managed the landing safely. To be marooned in this trackless waste was certain death. We were well into Siberia by now, more than a thousand miles from the nearest inhabitation. We could never cross this great plain on foot. Nor was it easy to see how we could possibly be rescued if we got ourselves into trouble. If a landing was impossible for us, it would be impossible for any plane sent out to our help. Yet we all felt something had to be done. Somehow we had to find out what this thing below us was. We could go back to base, of course, and make plans for tomorrow, or for the following week, but it was hard to see how this would get us any further.

One thing was favourable, there was almost no wind. This meant we could go down in a smooth gentle glide if we wanted to. Our Australian pilot was not to be put off. 'I'm going to have a crack at the bastard,' he said. 'We'll go down until our wheels touch, then I'll bring her up again. We ought to be able to tell from the hydraulic shock on the wheels whether we're dealing with soft or hard ground.'

Now we were down to a thousand feet, then quickly down to five hundred. The last seconds seemed interminably long. The jolt was much harder than I expected, really because the pilot didn't quite know where the surface was. As we came up again it needed no examination of the hydraulic system to know that we had hit hard ground.

Our line was to the north so as to avoid the glare of the Sun. After stabilizing the aircraft and checking the instruments we came down again. This time we made a normal landing. There would be nobody here to wheel a flight of steps out to the plane. We would have to hang a ladder of some sort. The crew got out a lightweight metal job. I was glad of this, because the rigidity of the metal would make the climb back into the plane reasonably easy. We opened the front hatch and let out the ladder. A couple of minutes later I was swinging down it.

I stepped gingerly on to the ground, then away from the ladder, and down on to my hands and knees. I ran a hand over the surface. It was completely smooth. I tried to dig into it with a fingernail, but it was quite resistant. The colours were more vivid down here. By turning round in a circle from the direction of the Sun in the south to the anti-sun in the north, and then back again to the south, it was possible to go through a whole cycle of changes. It was a vivid yellow towards the Sun, then green as one swivelled round towards the west, then

85

a pale blue in the north-west, purple in the north, and back through the same colours in a reverse order as one turned through east to the south again. It was the same wherever one stood.

I walked away from the plane to a distance of about three hundred yards. The difference between looking towards the plane and looking away from it was quite fantastic. Looking away from it one had no impression of scale whatsoever. It was impossible to know whether you were looking ten yards, a hundred yards, or even a hundred miles. The effect was bewildering and distinctly frightening. It was far more weird than the kind of white-out you sometimes get on a snowfield in the mountains. Yet as soon as you turned round, there was the plane – the whole scene jumped instantly into scale.

John came up to me.

'What do you make of it?' I asked.

'It's a kind of glass. We're on a huge glass plain stretching for thousands of miles.'

'But how, how the hell did it happen?'

'Heat. Heat from outside. The surface has been melted and fused. It's a kind of glass, rather like a tektite. except it's much more homogeneous, and far less brittle.'

'You said heat from the outside. What could cause that?'

'It's a bit like the glass you get after the explosion of a nuclear weapon. But there doesn't seem to be any radio-activity, from the Geiger counters in the plane.'

This explained the equipment I had seen John fiddling with during the flight.

'How far do you think it goes?'

'God knows. Perhaps all the way to China.'

'That's going to take out a big slice of the land area.'

'You know it's very strange...'

John stopped, as he always did, when he was in the middle of some important statement. Now he went on, 'How smooth it all is. You'd expect the surface to be scratched, by blown sand or bits of grit. It should have a short of sand-blasted, matt finish.' .

'You think that's important?'

'Well, it must mean there's never been any bits of sand or grit, there's no other explanation. The point I think is that everything's been melted, every damn last bit of surface rock. Nothing was left over.'

'If we follow up your idea about different parts of the Earth belonging to different ages, do you think this could refer to a time after a disastrous nuclear war?'

'It could, I suppose. If it were a few centuries or more afterwards, I suppose the radioactivity would mostly have died down. We'd better dig up a chunk of the stuff and take it back with us for analysis. That should tell us if there's any long-lived artificial radioactivity in it. Probably it isn't much good speculating until we know the facts.'

When we attempted to quarry the material we found the ground quite extraordinarily hard. We laughed at our fears about making a landing. The whole plain, millions of square miles of it, was just one ideal, perfect airstrip.

It began to grow chilly as the Sun fell lower in the west. We decided to eat a meal before taking off. After a short argument it was decided to have it out of doors. The food was handed down the ladder by the crew. Soon we were munching sandwiches and drinking hot coffee. We took a last walk around the plane. A quarter of an hour later we were back in the air. Turned towards the Sun we were on our homeward journey.

We managed just about to hold our own with the rotation of the Earth, so the Sun maintained its position pretty well constant in the sky as we flew westward. Scattered clouds began to appear, then there was a thicker cover below us. An hour and a half later we were back over eastern Germany. I wondered what furious interchange of messages was going on down there, what diplomatic activity.

It was about six o'clock when we landed at London airport. We were almost smothered by reporters and cameramen. A posse of police managed to make a way for us. It occurred to me that not one of the newshounds around us could have suspected, eerie and odd as this new world might seem to them, that we had come back from something still stranger and more remote.

We discovered there was no possibility of getting the plane serviced soon enough for us to be able to make another exploratory voyage the following day. So I returned for the night to my own apartments in London. I found Alex Hamilton glued to the television set. He asked me what I knew about the situation. I told him a little, not too much. Then I asked him for his opinion. He said it was very interesting that, with America out of the way and with Europe back in 1917, we were way ahead of Webern and Schoenberg. All we had to do was to murder all the musicians in Britain, to destroy all the libraries, and we would be made. I said I thought he was completely on the wrong lines. These new events called for an epic style, not for abstractionalism. At this he fell into one of his laughing fits. 'So you're thinking of reviving the Cologne piece.'

I said I was thinking of much more than that, but along the same lines. In fact I was bursting with ideas and would be glad of the following day to jot a few things down.

I made dinner while Alex went on watching TV. Afterwards we both watched it. The B B C seemed to have moved into France *en bloc*. They reported that the Prime Minister had seen the French Prime Minister, Monsieur Briand. According to the reports the French were proving difficult. They were insisting that honour be satisfied. Then we learnt the Germans were sending their Foreign Minister to London, a man of the name of Kuhlmann. The British commanders in the field had been replaced by modern officers who were preparing a general retreat from the trenches.

At this stage I must put my own experiences aside in order to relate at secondhand how it came about that the war situation in France simply collapsed like a pack of cards. First the men themselves, the ordinary fighting soldiers. In the last months of 1917 they were in a curious psychological state of mind. They had come to see the trenches as the real world, they had come to regard the situation back home as an unreal dream. It was as though they had walked out of the ordinary world into hell and now hell was the place which really counted. If they thought at all of the people back home, then apart from their families it was with a dull sullen hatred. This was true as much on the one side as the other. So when instructions came to cease from the horrible slaughter the men had not the slightest compunction about obeying. It was what they wanted anyway. It had been the *outside* that had been impelling them. Suddenly it seemed as if a miracle had happened somehow on the outside, which was the way it had to be. What they had gone through could only be made good by a miracle. They had paid enough in agony for any miracle. If there was little element of rationality in this point of view it was backed by intense emotion. To the men it was a heaven-sent deliverance. The psychological effect of discovering a hiatus of fifty years seemed more or less in tune with the horrors of the battlefield itself.

On the German side there was little will to continue the fight. Kuhlmann had in any case been on the point of proposing peace terms himself, similar to those which the British government now suggested. And the German High Command was shaken to its roots by the situation in the east and south. Nothing at that stage was known in Germany of the existence of the huge Plain of Glass, but all communication with the East had mysteriously ceased. The railway tracks to the east continued normally to Warsaw and somewhat beyond that. Every town, every village, down to the smallest hamlet, seemed to be entirely normal up to a certain point. Then it all simply vanished. The railway tracks ceased. The vegetation ceased. Not a single person could be found. It was just a complete desert. Those who knew these facts, and there were not many at this stage, had the bottom knocked out of their self-confidence. Hindenburg and Ludendorff knew of course, as did most of the High Command. It could only mean that what was being said in the west, in Britain, was true. Added to the already bad state of the war, to the privations in Germany, it was decisive. It was agreed that Hindenburg should travel to London for the proposed conference.

A cease fire was already in effect by the time the conference was held. The biggest card in the hand of the British government was of course the military weapons of 1966. The immediate problem was to bring the strength of those weapons over to the German mind. An actual physical demonstration was to be avoided if at all possible. But in the game of political manoeuvre it is known, at least in the world of 1966 it was known, that even the strongest card will have no effect unless you take steps to acquaint your opponents of its existence. There is little point in keeping a card secret and then playing it as a sudden surprise. Almost exactly the reverse. Playing a strong card always alters a situation so it is never the same at the end as it was at the beginning.

The problem was solved in a simple fashion. It was solved by using one of the most remarkable feats of 1966, but one quite unmilitary in character. It was done simply with a high fidelity gramophone. Delegates from the continent were ushered through a room in which an old-fashioned tinny machine, the sort you wind up, with a little horn, was playing. It wheezed out its feeble sounds as the delegates assembled in the conference room. The delegates were at first surprised at this apparent eccentricity. Then they were shattered by a sudden switch to full volume on the 1966 equipment.

All that needed to be done was to draw a simple analogy. The Prime Minister just pointed out that the weapons of his own day, of 1966, bore the same relation to the weapons being used in France, as did this new powerful gramophone to the little whining horn of 1917. He asked the German staff officers to compare their own weapons with those of the year 1860. Then perhaps they would understand how things stood. He wasn't telling them this in order to claim a victory. He wasn't interested in a victory as they would understand it. The important thing was to get down to a discussion of acceptable peace terms. All that was needed was a rational, reasonable approach to the problem. It was rather like a headmaster scolding a group of naughty boys.

Two days after our first flight of exploration we made a second one. Our aim was to discover the state of affairs in the Mediterranean, the Near East, and the Middle East. Our plan was to fly out over the Balkans, then over Turkey, Armenia, into Persia, and back via Palestine, Greece, and Italy. We wanted to find out how far to the south the great Plain of Glass extended. It was the same crew and personnel as before.

As we climbed aboard the plane I was in a divided state of mind. I had a host of musical ideas hammering away in my brain, but I was dead set to make the trip for I was utterly fascinated by the strange new geography of the Earth. Also I was baffled and intrigued by the psychological problems that were going to occur when the men from 1917 came home to the world of 1966. How were the two worlds to collaborate with each other? What would happen when a man, perhaps of thirty, back from the trenches, met his own son in the year 1966, his son at the age of sixty? And how of the strangest cases of all, those in which a man appeared twice, both young and old? Questions such as these seemed so weird and singular that I would have been astonished to learn as I walked up the steps into the aircraft that I was on the verge of a trip which would take me still farther away from the sane, stable world of a month ago. I still had no conception of how deep the waters were to run.

9 Andante con Moto

We flew out across the battlefields. From our height, about twenty-five thousand feet, the devastation had a pitiful aspect about it. After our flight across America, and our recent flight in the East, the scale here seemed very tiny. It was tragic to think so small a fragment of the Earth had cost so many lives.

Within an hour we were over central Germany, then over Austria–Hungary, as I supposed it must now be called. The sharpness of the transition in the Balkans was obscured by the mountainous country. By the time we emerged into the flat lands of Rumania all was changed. Gone were patterns of organized cultivation. Plainly the line of demarcation between 1917 and something quite different occurred somewhere in the Transylvanian Alps.

We came down low. There was no absence of vegetation here. It grew in abundance. It was all utterly out of control, without organization. It looked as though man had never set his hand on the forests and grasslands which lay below us.

We flew over the Black Sea to the Turkish coast. Not a single ship or craft of any kind did we see. It was the same story in Turkey, wild vegetation without any sign of human activity or interference.

By now I was greatly impressed by how vast the Earth really was compared to the limited regions of which I had any knowledge myself. At first the changes in these regions had seemed of enormous significance. Yet Europe had shifted by only fifty years, America by only a couple of hundred years or so. Over most of the Earth the times might well be utterly different.

We flew on over Armenia to the Caspian. Then on the far side of the Caspian we saw one of our objectives, the shining Plain of Glass. Evidently we were again near some line of demarcation. We found the actual line running just south of what used to be the Aral Sea. Of that sea there was not the slightest trace. We turned south in the direction of Tashkent and Samarkand. The glass gave way to sand quite suddenly as if the fusing agent had extended to a particular point and then no further. Here there was straightforward desert, sand.

We must have been somewhere near latitude 40° when we picked up the first traces of humanity. There was not much of it, only an occasional very tiny village. Yet we were enormously encouraged by this modest discovery. We found nothing at all in the place we took to be the site of Tashkent. So we turned west again with the intention of exploring Baghdad and the Tigris–Euphrates valleys. We found more scattered evidence of human habitations, all on a very tiny scale. Even before we reached Baghdad I think we realized we were not looking down on the world of 1917.

On the site of Baghdad – there could be no doubt about the site from the contours of the river below us – there was only a small collection of hovels. Again we found only minute villages on the banks of the great rivers. This was not a part of the world I had been in, or over, before. So I had no real standard of comparison. But there seemed more water than I would have expected. Our pilot was in no doubt of it himself:

'A bloody great swamp down there, almost like the mouth of the Ganges. Completely changed. Pity we don't have a flying boat.'

We flew quite low on two or three occasions but could see no people. Perhaps this was not surprising for anybody down there must surely have thrown themselves into hiding at the roar of the plane. Our failure to find anything of interest as we travelled back to the west depressed us more and more. Nothing was to be seen in Mesopotamia of the armies of 1917. We flew on towards Palestine. Our intention was to locate the city of Jerusalem. This we could easily do once we found the Dead Sea, simply by flying on a westerly course from the northern end of the Sea.

We missed the Dead Sea on our first run. Since we were operating on our compasses we could always expect to be a hundred miles off course due to the wind. We did indeed come over a large expanse of water but it was clear we had reached the Mediterranean. So we turned south along the coast of Palestine in the direction of Egypt. We kept on until the coastline turned due west. This we knew must be the neighbourhood of Gaza. From there we found the Dead Sea quite easily. We carried out our plan of flying west from the northern tip. In five minutes or so we were over what should have been Jerusalem. There seemed to be signs of habitation but once again it was just a few hovels. There was no sign of the city of David, captured around the year 1050 B.C. It was plain the Hebrews had not, and now never would, reach the lands below us. Into this new world Christ would not be born.

We headed out over the Mediterranean. Very soon we were over the wine-dark seas of Greece. My reveries were sharply interrupted by a sudden grip on the arm:

'My god, look down there.'

The sea was breaking around a headland twenty thousand feet below us. Standing proudly on the headland was a temple. At once we were all animated. We flew round in circles coming lower and lower.

'Look, it's complete, it's not a ruin.'

'Where do you reckon we are?' I asked the pilot.

'I think we're just south of Athens.'

John had been looking at the chart. 'It fits the Attic peninsular. There's this island here off the east coast. Its shape fits that long one down there, doesn't it?'

There wasn't any doubt about it. We flew lower and lower. Now we could just make out people below us. They were running to the temple. I realized it was the temple of Sounion.

We said nothing as we turned up the coast to the north-west. It took only a few minutes before we were over Athens. Standing complete on the Acropolis was the Parthenon. Close by was an amphitheatre full of people. The city was not very large but at least it was a city. Whatever the time was down there it obviously had little to do with the twentieth century. The time had to be somewhere between the date of construction of the Parthenon, which I remembered to be about 450 B.C., and the date at which the temple at Sounion fell into ruin, which it must have done in the first centuries A.D. There seemed little doubt that we were looking down on the Greece of classical times.

We would have liked to have flown around for a long time, to have come as low as we dared, but we all realized it would be better not to do so. The people down there would see the great bird in the skies as a visitation from the gods. There would be panic and a wailing and gnashing of teeth. The sooner we were away the better. So regretfully we headed west towards Corinth. Naturally there was no canal cutting through the narrow neck of land which separates the Peloponnese from the land to the north. We saw a multitude of small boats as we flew along the Gulf, propelled it seemed by human muscle power, by oarsmen.

A further surprise was in store for us. Very naturally we were heading for Rome. We were doing so in the full expectation of it being classical times everywhere throughout the Mediterranean. The situation in Rome would allow us to date the epoch more closely. We were due for a sharp disappointment for over the Italian mainland there was nothing but vegetation. We flew on and on and it was the same everywhere. No city of Rome at all. No towns, villages, or hamlets. Only as we came north of the Alps did the wild country change. Quite abruptly we were in a modern society with its towns and streets and its factories. It was probably 1917 down there but we all felt we had suddenly come back to our own times. It was the same all the way from Switzerland across France. Then we were over the English Channel. It was hard to believe as we flew over the neat fields of Kent that the other regions of the Earth were so grotesquely changed.

To say it felt like waking from a dream is an admitted cliché yet there was a dreamlike quality about it all. Even now, I thought as we moved in to land, we have seen only a fraction of the Earth. We don't really know the Glass Plain extends right through China. We had no idea of the situation in Africa, or in South America, or anywhere in the southern hemisphere for that matter.

After the sandy deserts of the Middle and Near East, after the missing city of Jerusalem, Greece had seemed real enough. Now I was back in London it all seemed wildly ridiculous. Could one seriously credit that out there it might still be the third, fourth, or fifth century B.C.? Yet the fifth century B.C. had been just as real and sharp as 1966.

I had dinner the following night with John. We discussed at length our next moves. It was clear the flights of discovery had to go on without hindrance or delay. It was imperative to get a general idea of the new layout of the whole Earth. One of us at least must continue on those trips. The problem was to decide whether we should both go or whether we should split up, one to continue the general survey, the other to investigate details, perhaps details of the situation in Greece. This would have to be done with the greatest care. The Greeks would not be alarmed by the arrival of strangers, provided they came in a fashion that seemed normal, by boat from the sea. But not in a modern boat with thumping engines. John told me preparations were already being made along these lines. The government had asked the navy to send in an expedition. Did I want to be included in the party? If I did it would be necessary to drop my name in the right quarter, and without delay. I said I would sleep on it. We agreed to meet again at lunch on the morrow.

The decision was an awkward one pretty well evenly balanced. I was completely fascinated at the prospect of seeing classical Greece at first hand. This would be the real thing not a cruise organized two thousand years after the event. Yet I had the feeling I would be pushing myself out of the main stream of events. The trip must surely be a leisurely one taking weeks if not months. I would lose contact with John. I would hence lose my entrée to the high-stepping circles in which I had moved of late. This was entirely a matter of unbridled curiosity not at all of snobbery. I wanted to know what was going on. Quite clearly the intricate dealings between Britain and Europe would be utterly intriguing to observe at close quarters.

Ironically these considerations were grossly wide of the mark for the mainstream of events was not at all where I supposed it to be. As it came about my decision made no difference to my arriving at the true mainstream, but in the ultimate outcome it did make a critical difference, that of my arriving independently not by John's much more direct route. No thoughts of this kind were in my mind of course when at last I came down on the side of the Grecian expedition. It was music which swayed the balance. For one thing, here was the chance to settle all the controversy and arguments about ancient music. For another, I was more and more feeling the need of leisure to give expression to my own creative impulses. The flights, the discussions, marvellously intriguing in themselves, were consuming the whole of my time and energies. A reduction of tempo was needed.

When I told John of my decision he was a little doubtful:

'Things have changed a bit in the last twenty-four hours, I'm afraid. The government is getting itself bogged down more and more with the European situations. They're really not in a position to give much priority to the Greek business. It was agreed yesterday to keep things pretty well on ice for the time being.'

'You mean the expedition is off?'

'Not entirely but it's only going to be a small show.'

I have an obstinate streak in me. When I'm thinking about any issue I like to hear the opinions of other people. I like to collect as much information as possible. But once I've made a decision I like to stick to it. Once I've made up my mind I hate to be 'advised'. I passed off John's entirely good-tempered warning. I'd made my decision. I told him so and without further ado he regarded the matter as closed.

'They've put the whole thing under an old naval boy, Admiral Cochrane. You'll be hearing from him pretty soon.'

Throughout lunch I could see John was bubbling over with something or other. Until my problem was out of the way he wouldn't say what it was. Then he chuckled and let it all out:

'Remember we were talking the other day about what would happen when a man in 1966 came face to face with himself in 1917? Well, it's happened, in a way.'

'How d'you mean, in a way?'

'Not a direct confrontation, as of yet.'

'Go on.'

'A most exalted member of the government. They've managed to hush it up so far, but it's bound to come out.'

'Why shouldn't it come out?'

'They're still keeping the identity of the exalted member secret but I don't think I would need more than one guess.'

'I wish I could guess what it is you're driving at.'

'We were thinking in terms of a man from the trenches coming back and meeting himself. Remember?'

'For heaven's sake, out with it!'

'It's not the man that's come back from France, it's the mother.'

'I'm getting in deeper, into a bog.'

'The mother was in the VAD. She's come back. So the son has met his mother, aged twenty, thirty years or so younger than he is.'

'Very touching I would imagine.'

'You're still not with it, I'm afraid. The point is the mother was, more properly *is*, of a kindly disposition. She took pity on a young officer. Natural enough in the circumstances, considering what's been going on in France. In a curious way, death always tends to breed life.'

The preposterous implication hit me. 'You mean the *alter ego* is still in the womb!'

'Right. You could hardly imagine a confrontation more curious than that, could you? I thought I'd covered most of the possibilities but this one got completely past me.'

On this ludicrous note John and I parted, the one of us as it turned out to follow the high road, the other the low road. Not to Scotland, to somewhere very different.

10 Entr'acte

While the events of this narrative were still happening it was
difficult to separate the trivial from the important. It was also
difficult to perceive any general structure underlying the whole
affair. Yet looking backward it is easy to see that the structure
was rather like the two acts of a play with each act divided
into two scenes. The experiences in Scotland, California, and
Hawaii constituted Act 1, Scene 1, the juxtaposition of the
Britain of 1966 with the Europe of 1917 constituted Act 1,
Scene 2.

The second act remains for me to describe. My point here is
that the two acts were connected by occurrences whose very
ordinariness quite concealed the inexorable transition which
took place from the still more or less normal world of Act 1 to
the utterly new and strange world of Act 2.

Outwardly nothing more was involved than the transport by
sea of a small party from Britain to Greece. In the spring of
1966 it had been easy to breakfast in London, to lunch in
Athens, the flight by air took a mere two hours. By 28 September, the day we left Portsmouth Harbour, there were no
flights. The number of planes now existing in the whole world
was quite few. There were no airports in Greece any more.
There were no rail tracks, no roads even, across the Alps.
Every available ship had been diverted to the European cross-
ings. There was no simple way of reaching Greece any more,
and those ways which apparently were open, like our sea
route, became closed only a few days later. We crossed a
barrier on 30 September as we steamed south off the coast of
Portugal. The following day, 1 October, would have been too
late.

The day after my last talk with John Sinclair I had a call
from Admiral Cochrane. I learned the party was to be under
the 'command' of a Captain Morgan Evans, a one-time
classical scholar of Balliol. An anthropologist, also with a

knowledge of ancient Greek and also from Oxford, had been chosen. I believed I had heard of Anna Feldman, a formidable battle-axe as I recalled. Two other members from an intelligence unit remained to be assigned to the expedition. The general idea was to take a naval vessel to a point south of Greece and just west of Crete. A small boat would then be launched and would continue to the Greek mainland. The boat would be equipped both with sail and with auxiliary engines. Following a discussion of such details the Admiral suggested the whole party might meet for dinner that night, would I be available?

Outwardly there was nothing about Anna Feldman to suggest the tempestuous virago, inwardly it might be another matter. To the eye she seemed a pleasant-looking woman in the middle thirties. I took immediately to Morgan Evans. I judged him to be about fifty. I also judged him to have a real Welsh temperament underlying the reserve of the naval officer. Of the chaps from intelligence there was still no sign – I presumed they were lying doggo until the last possible moment.

Dinner was over before nine o'clock. It seemed a bit early to break up so I suggested we might all proceed to my apartments after making the usual apologies for untidiness and disarray. We flagged a taxi and drove through the nearly empty streets.

I had been chosen for the expedition because of my presence on the original discovery flight. Only when the Admiral noticed sheets of manuscript scattered over my piano did he realize I was a musician. The old boy turned out to have a regular passion for Schubert. I started with the *Rosamunde* ballet music, then the Opus 90 impromptus. Whenever I play any composer's works I always become increasingly enthusiastic as I go on. More and more Schubert poured forth, the Schubert of the popular image, with wonderful tunes and rustling accompaniments. Then I remembered the other Schubert, the Schubert of fire and grandeur, a Schubert almost unknown to the world at large. I hunted quickly among stacks of music. At last I found what I wanted, the three posthumous sonatas. I started on the F sharp Minor.

What can one say of the Andantino in this sonata? Why call it Andantino, why refer to a shattering achievement as if it were a child's piece? How the devil did the man do it? How did the composer of *Rosamunde* suddenly become the composer of the F sharp Minor? How did extreme subtlety suddenly become combined with a consuming flame of passion and tragedy?

I continued to ponder these questions in the weeks and months ahead. I came at last to understand far more of what I now believe to be the essence of music, more than I ever gleaned from my teachers or from my own endeavours as a pianist and as a composer. Great music has nothing really to do with technique or even with an honest determination. Technique, skill, experience, determination, all these are necessary factors, but they are only peripheral. For every musician who has achieved anything truly great there must have been hundreds with adequate technique and keen determination. The missing component was the inner well-spring of emotion. Unless the inner fires burn with a fierce intensity the rest serves only as a gloss, like an automobile standing there with its paintwork and chrome all polished and shining but without any engine to drive it.

I have always had barely hidden doubts about much of contemporary music. I understand abstract music, I know what composers are trying to do: I have myself written quite a lot of abstract music but always I have had a sense of unease. Now I see why. Abstract music represents an attempt by very highly skilled people to eliminate from music the essential component which they themselves lack, the emotional fires. Abstract music is an attempt to make technique sufficient, an indefensible position I think. For why on this basis should one not be a mathematician? Music is the wrong profession for the purely abstract.

The difficulty of course is that you can't conjure emotion, sexual emotion perhaps, but not the deeper emotions. Schubert wrote those posthumous sonatas because he was impelled to do so. But not by thoughts of box office or of the plaudits of the world. There must indeed have seemed every likelihood that his manuscripts would even be thrown away, that every note would be lost to oblivion. Yet this was of no consequence, for Schubert wrote in his last year, with the figure of Death standing clearly over him. These sonatas were his dialogues with Death. They were his inquiry, a musician's inquiry, into the meaning of life and death. The world, in the sense of 'success' or of 'recognition', had no part in them.

Perhaps here we have a clue to why the Andantino was so named. Perhaps it did seem like a child's piece when taken in such a grim dialogue. I played the Andantino with very little pedal. At the end the Admiral was so affected that for a moment I thought he had been overcome by a heart attack – in a sense he had, but of a favourable kind.

The evening with Schubert had two consequences. For one, everybody wanted a small piano to be included in the expedition's equipment. Stowing a piano aboard a ten-ton yacht would create problems but the Admiral was keenly determined on their solution.

Two days went by in which we found ourselves hanging around still waiting for the chaps from intelligence. Cochrane at last told me he was having 'difficulties'. Intelligence was more than fully occupied in Europe. It was now felt impossible to release anybody for our 'show'. This brought home very sharply the extent to which I had allowed myself to be shunted on to a side-track, very much confirming John's warning. Yet the obstinate streak in me was still dominant. I had no thought of withdrawing. I asked the Admiral if he would come along himself. Regretfully, the answer was the same, European commitments. So rather as an afterthought I asked if there would be any objection to a friend of mine, another musician, being included. This was how it came about that Alex Hamilton was aboard when at last we steamed out of Portsmouth Harbour. The second outcome of the Schubert evening.

Our ship was not very prepossessing, it was a workaday ship. It had to be because of the equipment needed to launch our boat. By the evening of 30 September we were off the coast of Portugal. The days slipped placidly away. Beyond Gibraltar now, we steamed steadily east towards the isles of Greece. We would sit on deck until far into the night. The sea was calm. Surrounded by the darkened waters, stars filling the sky, anything seemed possible. Jason and the Argonaut might have glided by.

During the next days we familiarized ourselves with the gear on the yacht. Launching was a somewhat hectic process. We anchored in as shallow water as the captain dared. Then the men built a good-sized slipway. I had visions of the yacht getting out of control as it went down into the sea but everything passed off quite well. Held on powerful ropes, the boat moved slowly foot by foot down to the water, not at all the swift dramatic launching I had expected. With its auxiliary engines started, the crew quickly had it away from the edge of our ship to a safe distance. The last step before we ourselves embarked was to check with our captain on the rendezvous we had arranged for two months hence. Greece might well be flooded by tourists and newsmen long before two months were up. Yet if this should not happen we intended to make our departure as inconspicuously as possible. We would simply reverse the procedure of our arrival. We had sufficient fuel to return to the neighbourhood of Crete where we would be met by our naval escort.

It was early morning when our yacht was launched. By nine o'clock we were on our way. We waved good-bye and within an hour we were alone in an open sea.

Really all we had to do was to run almost exactly due north. Inevitably this would bring us to the Attic peninsula. From there we could navigate simply by eye. Timing was something of a difficulty. Arriving at a modern port in the evening with modern electrical illumination was one thing. Arriving at an ancient port more or less in darkness was another. We decided it would be better not to rush things, to go slowly and to arrive the following morning. This we could easily do by changing to sail. There was a lot of sense in this because we needed practice with the sails. We were distinctly clumsy in our work. We kept the engines running at low revolutions until we got the hang of it.

By nightfall we had been going nine hours. I reckoned I must have come some fifty miles. We took down the sails and started the engines again. Our course now was somewhat to the east of north. Twelve more hours at five knots should put us just about right, providing the weather held. Luckily it did. I slept very well indeed considering the circumstances and the occasion. In a queer way it had all come to assume the aspect of an everyday experience. Saturated by the new and the strange, I was ready simply to accept whatever chanced to come along.

I woke to the smell of cooking bacon. Anna had a primus stove going. Soon I was washed and dressed and munching happily. Then it was time to stop the engines and to go back to sail. This time we managed with less incident and argument.

Except that Alex almost got himself knocked overboard by a swinging boom. In the harassment of the moment I reflected that he might keep away from his sudden exits, at least for the next few hours.

By ten o'clock we could see land all the way ahead of us. The island of Hydra lay on the left. This was as it should be. Throughout the morning we sailed on, coming ever nearer to the coast ahead.

Now occurred the first event to signal our passage to a new world and a new era. We came up on a boat such as I had never seen before. It was of about the same size as our own but undecked. Although it had a single large crude sail the main contribution to its speed came from oarsmen, about ten to each side of the boat. We started the engines as a precaution, for we had no wish to fall foul of a pirate ship. Then we went in to hailing distance. There was an interchange between the men in the boat and Morgan, of which I didn't understand a word. We accelerated away from them. When we were about a quarter of a mile ahead I asked, 'What did they say?'

'Only that they're on their way to Athens too. I said we were strangers which must have seemed pretty obvious. I said we'd go in ahead of them.'

'I suppose it wasn't the right occasion to find out what's going on?'

'I've been thinking about that, you know. We'll have to be extremely careful in our inquiries. Remember the Greeks date their years from 776 B.C., the year in which they started the Olympic Games. The best thing will be to ask them for an explanation of how they count the years.'

Then Morgan and Anna fell into an impassioned discussion about what the men in the boat had been saying. Classical scholars of the twentieth century were going to have their troubles, it seemed. Suddenly Alex gripped my arm and pointed ahead. We were getting quite close in now to what I took to be the port of Piraeus.

'Look, aren't those the Long Walls?'

We were all gazing at the seven or eight miles of unbroken wall, a wall that swept from near the sea away to the north-east. Athens we knew must lie at the northern end.

'The wall is complete,' whispered Anna. 'It must mean we're somewhere around the time of Pericles.'

Now came the worst of our problems, to tie up the boat without using the engines. The harbour lay ahead. We could see more open boats, charmingly and somewhat impracticably designed. We took the simple line of taking down sail, throwing out an anchor, and waiting for the people on shore to come to us. This worked out exactly as one might have expected. Soon there was an excited throng at the water edge obviously wondering at the strange lines of the new vessel which had appeared from the sea. Within a few moments half a dozen boats were rowed out to us. Morgan somehow managed to convey the idea that we wanted a tow to a safe spot. A dozen or more men took our rope. With much argument and laughter they hauled us about two hundred and fifty yards to a sheltered spot where there was a draught of about ten feet. Once again we put down anchor. Morgan and Alex rowed ashore in our dinghy. They made fast with a rope. Within a few minutes we were all safely landed. I realized now that our story of being strangers from the north, the land of giants in Greek lore, would seem entirely true. I was a full head taller than any of these people.

11 Vivace

It would be easy to become deeply involved in the very many detailed differences between modern society and the times in which we were now immersed, but an encyclopaedic description of the situation would only obscure the wood by the trees. It was the differences of principle which really counted.

Take the height of the people. I found it hard not to think of them all as children, simply because they were ten inches to a foot shorter than I was, a difference of only some fifteen per cent when you think about it. My reaction came because I was conditioned to think of significantly smaller people as children. Yet these people were just as clever, just as much driven by strong emotion, by the desire for power, love, intellectual achievement, as we ourselves were.

Everything about us was hand-made, every movement – at any rate on the land – was provided by muscle, either animal or human. While most things were meaner, evidence of better taste was to be seen in almost every article. Nothing in our modern society could exceed, or perhaps even equal, the finest women's dresses I was to see here. Yet these dresses demanded enormous effort, a far greater fraction of the productivity of the community, than was the case in modern society. This meant that fine clothing could only be worn by privileged persons and then only on special occasions. The everyday dress of the average citizen was rough and crude by our modern machine standards. It would have been impossible for it to be otherwise in a society of such limited resources.

The same was true of the buildings. On the whole people lived in houses little better than hovels. Only the wealthiest members of the community approached what we would call average middle-class comfort. Yet public buildings, the Parthenon, were of a magnificence our modern society could not equal at all. Indeed the situation was exactly reversed in the world of 1966. Private homes could be spacious and tasteful.

Public buildings, public offices, hospitals, the whole gamut of state enterprises, were nearly always painfully sordid.

It took a little time both to notice and to get used to these differences. Immediately after our landing we were concerned to ensure the safety of our boat and to see our few important possessions adequately locked away below deck. No doubt hundreds of pairs of inquisitive hands would work themselves over every exposed inch of the yacht. Yet it seemed doubtful they would actually break in through the closed hatchways. At any rate we decided to take the risk. There was no car or bus to carry us the eight miles to Athens. We simply walked along the great fortified wall of the city.

We were met three miles out by civic dignitaries. I could tell nothing of what was said, for in the beginning I had only the crudest knowledge of the language, picked up from Morgan and Anna on the few days of our voyage from Britain. Morgan took on the task of explaining our position. He spoke clearly and slowly. His inflexion provided the populace at large with a considerable source of amusement. Yet his commanding height, combined with a Welsh flair for erudition, had a disarming effect on his audience. Clearly we were well received.

All I could tell was that we were escorted under favourable circumstances into the city. We arrived at length at an open area where about a thousand people had quickly gathered at the news of our arrival. The place of our congregation was a discussion arena, of the name Agora, I learnt later. There seemed to be nothing for it but that Morgan should give an account of the manner of our journey from the north, through the Pillars of Hercules, the western Mediterranean, and thence to Athens. I was surprised at the length of his speech. Only later did I realize that time was a commodity not in short supply in this community. It would have been taken as an insult, when so many were gathered together, to have spoken tersely. Morgan knew this from his classical studies. Later he told me he addressed the throng something along the following lines:

At this time of the year the days in the north are short, the Sun lies low in the sky. Our fields and our houses are battered by the strong wind which blows everlastingly from the west. Rain clouds fill the sky with an ever-present threat of violent storms. So you may understand the thoughts of my countrymen turn often to the lands of the south, for it is a belief among our people that southern lands are warmer, winds lighter, that in every way the natural elements are less destructive of human comfort. It was to discover whether this was so that we commenced our journey.

I give only this short example of Morgan's discursive style. It would be painful to attempt even a partial repetition of his speech, of the manner and construction of our vessel, of the nature of our rivers and harbours, of the terrors of the open sea. He described our farewell to our native land giving them a Greek version of John of Gaunt's speech from Richard II. Then the sights we had seen on our journey, the birds and fishes, the Rock of Gibraltar. The words flowed on and on until I wondered if he was intent on talking the whole day away. Not a sound came from the audience. Although, as I say, there was upward of a thousand of them, everyone seemed able to hear. The excellent acoustic properties of Greek theatres, always such a marvel to the modern world, came from the fact that the spoken word, discussion and argument, had absolute top priority. In days before the microphone and loud speaker, acoustics simply had to be good. Soon I was to realize that to be able to speak clearly, with persuasion and reason, was equivalent to power in this city.

Everybody listened in rapt attention. I expected a barrage of questions at the end. Yet there were no questions, only applause. Later I realized that questions were regarded as perfectly proper in any argument or disputation, but questions were not asked at the end of a free speech.

It was not until about two in the afternoon that we left the Agora. We were taken to the house of one of the wealthiest inhabitants. A meal had been prepared. For the first time I was aware of the existence of slaves. Not in any violent way but by the manner in which certain people were addressed; the voice tone is unmistakable in any language. The food was simple but of good quality. The mutton with which we were served was very far from being the everyday diet of the average Greek. The bread likewise was something important and precious. The bread was served by itself as a separate course. We were given a cup of liquid which turned out to be olive oil. Luckily I have a liking for olive oil and so did not suffer the torments which afflicted Alex. The meat was served with wine, which soon cut away the greasy taste of the oil. The oil in its turn prevented any strong intoxication. The meal ended with fresh fruit of a quality I had never tasted before.

Through the meal Morgan and Anna had of necessity to take on themselves the whole interchange of information. I noticed there was no interest at all in what we did. I was never asked what I was, and I think the notion of my being a musician would have baffled them. Everybody here was what they wanted to be, what they were interested in. This was among the leisured classes, for it was taken for granted that we ourselves must be wealthy persons. Only the wealthy could contemplate a voyage such as we had made. Our hosts were concerned with the structure of the seas beyond the Pillars of Hercules, with what we believed about the nature of the world. How was our political life organized?

They didn't like the idea of elected representatives of the people. To them it was important that every free adult member of the community should be permitted to vote on every specific issue. It was impossible to explain that the very size of our population precluded their own democratic system. Morgan pointed out that our people were scattered in many cities, that it was impossible for them to be constantly travelling in order to discuss things together. It was essential for each city to appoint its own representatives and for the representatives of all the cities to confer together. I was surprised and rather alarmed by the serious, chilled manner in which this was received. The idea of a number of cities working together on terms of equality was apparently repugnant to them.

After the meal our party divided up. We were taken separately to the house of some wealthy person. My own host got little out of me, I am afraid, for in the beginning I could do no more than smile and nod. It is true my ears were already picking up the sounds of this new language. I was listening keenly, and watching the manner in which the sounds were made by the mouth, but it would be several months yet before I would be able to converse with any freedom. It came as a surprise to find how soon after sundown everybody retired for the night. I quickly became used to this aspect of life, however. Indeed, a reverse reaction set in, it became difficult to understand why the possession of artificial light persuades modern society to outphase the day. Within a week I came to think of the practice of staying up, out of bed, after the Sun has long since set, and of then staying in bed after the Sun has long since risen, as entirely absurd.

The following day I managed to convey to my host that there were certain things on the ship I would like to fetch. Lots of people wanted to help. Nobody seemed to think anything of a sixteen-mile walk, eight miles there and eight miles back.

What I wanted was the piano. It was a devil of a problem to get it out of the yacht's cabin on to the shore. There were willing hands in plenty. We took it to pieces as far as we could. It was not particularly difficult to get the smaller pieces across, the legs, the keyboard, and so forth. The trouble came with the main iron frame. Yet it is surprising what a sufficient amount of muscle power will do. I was haunted by the fear of the whole thing ending up at the bottom of ten feet of clear water. But these people knew how to lift weights. Their major buildings were an astonishing tribute to their abilities in this respect. The essential thing was not to be in a hurry. So far as possible they never made a move which could not be reversed. The first thing was to distribute the weight over the maximum possible area. The trouble with an iron frame taken by itself is the sheer concentration of its weight. So what was done was to build a kind of wooden raft to which the frame was securely tied with many ropes. Then on to the raft long poles were securely lashed, so the whole thing could be moved more or less like a passenger in a sedan chair. The long poles allowed a dozen men or more to take part in the lifting operation. First they lifted it from the yacht into one of the big open boats. Then they manoeuvred the boat close enough to the shore for men wading to reach it. After this the rest was easy. They managed the full eight miles back to the city in less than three hours. I spent the afternoon and the following day carefully reassembling the parts with an apparent infinity of helpers.

Tuning was something I wasn't at all used to. I had taken the precaution of bringing a number of forks, which ensured the fundamentals of the job. Then I simply trusted to my ear. There isn't any difficulty in knowing when a piano is in tune or out of tune. The difficulty is to know exactly what to do if it's out of tune. You have to judge what move you must make next. My advantage over a professional tuner was time, I had plenty of it, I didn't have to rush on to the next job in order to earn my living. In fact I took the whole afternoon of the first day and the following day before I had it to my liking.

At this point I should mention that Alex plays the violin with great competence but like a solitary drinker he would usually only play to himself. Yet I noticed he had brought his fiddle with him. In fact I'd been quite envious of the ease with which he packed it and the ease with which he got it ashore. It struck me how much the shape and size and weight of musical instruments are related to their origin. Violins, easily carried, from itinerant players. Flutes and reed instruments, also easily carried, the possessions of wandering shepherds. Drums, not easily carried, the prerogative of courts, of pomp and circumstance. Double basses and pianofortes, not easily carried, the inventions of later ages when transport had become highly organized. I was acutely aware that, whereas Alex would be able to carry his violin from house to house, city to city, into the country if need be, I would be more or less stuck here in Athens with my piano.

Of course there were compensating advantages. Harmony and counterpoint could both be given full range, or nearly full range, on a piano. On the violin only simple harmonies could be achieved, and then only by superb playing. Counterpoint was hardly to be thought of on a single violin. This wasn't the end of it. I had the whole of musical literature, not merely piano music, but symphonies and quartets, available to me.

I began to play the second afternoon of our arrival. So many people gathered around that it was necessary to move out of doors, into a fairly extensive courtyard. My audience was obviously amazed at the intricacy of the whole thing. I realized, as it turned out correctly, that their ears were not tuned to complex sounds. So I kept to simple lines. It was natural for me to play a selection of operatic arias. I played just what came into my head. There was a considerable proportion of Mozart in it. Naturally I was curious as to how the music would be received by my audience. In a quite strange way, mainly with argument. At the end of a number there would be a crowding round the piano, there would be a lot of gesticulation, and there would be a great deal of talk. I was soon to realize that the two things taken most seriously here were war and speech. Both were far ahead of sex in the estimation of the people. In fact sex was like food, a regular necessity but not to be fussed about. Talk ranged over the whole gamut, from private groups of half a dozen people up to the great oratorical speeches to many thousands. An immense amount of time and care went into the big speeches, for as I have already remarked persuasion was equivalent here to power. You were not permitted to murder a neighbour whom you might detest, but if you could persuade your fellow citizens that your neighbour was a danger to the community then the city itself would turn on him, imprison him, exile him, deprive him of his rights and property, and in extreme cases might even execute him. The gift of the gab was a matter of no small importance. It extended even to music.

It wasn't long before two flutes and a lyre appeared. They were very simply but well made. A sturdy, bright-faced young fellow of eighteen or nineteen began to pipe away on one of the flutes. Soon he was joined by a girl at the lyre. She used a small piece of wood to pluck the strings. The music was in a simple 4/4 rhythm. It was highly modal in its melodic structure. That is to say the notes used depended on the pitch of the octave in which the melody happened to lie.

Let me add a word here on different systems of musical composition. They all depend on some kind of restriction. In the modern style, modern in the sense of the twentieth century, there is no restriction at all on the notes you can use. They all have equal weight. The restriction comes on the order in which the notes are to be played, the restrictions being determined in part by the order which the composer himself lays down at the beginning of his composition, and in part by certain standard rules. In tonal music, the music of the eighteenth and nineteenth centuries, the restriction comes on the notes to be used. Only seven out of the twelve notes in the octave have equal weight. The other five appear only occasionally as accidentals. The manner in which the restriction to seven notes is made is also subject to certain rules, your particular choice being called the key in which you elect to operate. Once you have restricted yourself by a choice of key you are free to arrange your seven notes in any order you please. You are free to use the same seven notes in any octave you may please. And at any time you may change your restriction, you may modulate into another key. The style of this Greek music was more akin to the key system than to the modern serialization. It restricted the notes to be used to seven, but you had no freedom over which seven, you couldn't choose your key to suit yourself. The seven notes were decided by the pitch of your octave. I think the practice probably came from the manufacture of the instruments themselves. The instruments produced certain notes better than others, unlike the piano which produces all its notes equally. The general effect was rather plaintive to an ear grown accustomed to the key system.

The young man turned over his flute to someone else, took hold of one of the girls, and began to dance. The motions were simple, rather static, but graceful none the less. When they had finished I went back to the piano and played three or four waltzes. There was much laughter as several of the bolder spirits tried to find the right steps. I stopped the music to give them a short demonstration, first alone, then of the positions of the two partners, with my young friend's girl, then of the real speed of the dance with an imaginary partner. Back at the piano I played the dances at first quite slowly, then with increasing speed. The dancing was more or less a fiasco but everybody enjoyed it for all that.

This was the beginning of a reputation which I soon acquired for myself and of which I shall have more to say later on. It was made clear that I didn't have to go to bed by myself if I didn't want to, but I did want to. To me, it was still not much more than a month since the tragic affair in Los Angeles. The memory of those few whirlwind days was still sharp and clear. In what had started as a more or less casual liaison I had perhaps made the mistake of giving too much of myself. At any rate I was still numb from the sharp catastrophic end of a passionate situation. I saw it would be a good idea to spread the intelligence that I was suffering from a grievous bereavement. I resolved to ask Morgan to put this story around the following day.

Before dropping off to sleep I mused on one small item of information I had gleaned from the talk around me. The young flute player's name had been Xenophon. Was this the Xenophon who was later to rescue a whole Greek army from disaster in Mesopotamia? I had no means of knowing how common the name might be so there was no clear answer. I had also discovered the name of my host, Andocides. I had a feeling the name should mean something to me and I resolved to ask Morgan about it on the morrow.

As it turned out I had no need to seek out the others, they were waiting for me the following morning. Morgan knew now exactly where he was. He knew the year and the time of year. It was 425 B.C.

'Man, we're right in the middle of it.'

I was still sleepy and wondered vaguely what it was we were in the middle of.

'The war, the war between Athens and Sparta.'

'Then why are there so many men about?'

'Because winter is coming on. These things run more or less on a strict time-table. You know we ought to do something about it, to put an end to it.'

He was very excited, understandably so. To the classical scholar the fall of Athens in the Peloponnesian War must seem utterly tragic. Yet this was a different world now. It was inconceivable that a war between two tiny Greek cities, with a population of only a few hundred thousand, would be permitted to drag on year after year. The situation was tragic all right but not in the sense Morgan seemed to think. He had immersed himself so much in classical literature, he was thinking so much in the ancient Greek language, that he seemed to have forgotten the barbarians from the north who would soon be arriving here. Soon this delicate civilization around us would collapse like a house of cards. Financially the people would do all right of course. There were not very many of them, only a million or two, I suppose. With their great tourist attractions, the standard of living would rise sharply, but the civilization and culture would soon be lost. Above all the confidence would be lost. This was the problem, not the problem of Athens and Sparta.

An odd thought occurred to me, what was it Morgan had said? We must do something to stop it. Wasn't that exactly what the Prime Minister had said, about the situation in Europe? In many ways we had the same situation here. A disastrous war knocking the stuffing out of both sides. In one place the year was 1917, in the other 425 B.C., but the pattern was really the same.

Morgan had now drawn up a list of prominent Athenians, men whom sooner or later we could expect to find in the city.

Socrates, Euripides, and Aristophanes were the names which meant most to me. At the distance of the twentieth century these men seemed more or less contemporaries. From Morgan's list I realized their respective ages were forty-five, fifty-five and twenty. 'Socrates is out of town. With the army in the north.'

In the next few days the general picture of what was happening gradually came into focus. This was indeed a city at war. We had been deceived into thinking otherwise because the fighting during the last few months had gone almost uniformly in favour of Athens. Standing out above a number of minor victories, there had been a major success at Pylos, on the far side of the Peloponnesus. A Spartan peace offer had been refused, and the peace offer had been followed by the arrival in Athens of a couple of hundred Spartan prisoners. It was a pathetically minor affair compared to what had been happening in Europe, yet it accounted for the apparently carefree aspect of the city. Nobody had any doubt that the war with Sparta would soon be brought to a victorious conclusion, least of all the commanding officers. Yet we knew that if it were to follow its own course the war would last for another twenty years and would result in the defeat of Athens. But how was one to convince them of this?

Morgan, with the enthusiasm of a Welsh revivalist, made a shot at it. He made more progress than might have been supposed, partly because of his impressive height, partly because he knew from his historical studies more or less what the Spartan envoys had said when they had come to request peace earlier in the year. The coincidence between his arguments, the arguments of a complete foreigner, and the entirely reasonable point of view of the Spartans, made an impression. It accorded with one section of Athenian opinion. But it fell foul of the influential generals. After their recent success at Pylos, these men, Cleon and his friends, were riding the top of the wave. There was little Morgan could really do except make us thoroughly unpopular. Indeed our respective hosts began to find us something of an embarrassment. With some relief they seized on my suggestion that we acquire a house of our own. Everybody, friends and those not so friendly, made an effort to get us installed in congenial quarters. We were given half a dozen slaves and left to look after ourselves. So much for Morgan's preachings.

I didn't have much enthusiasm myself for this stop-the-war project. I was quite convinced that things would change drastically and catastrophically for the reasons I have already given. What I did have strong feelings about, however, were the slaves. I had no objection to hiring the middle-aged man and woman, the three girls, and the boy, as paid servants. So I conveyed to them that henceforward they were freed, although they could continue to work for a wage if they so pleased. All but the boy decided to stay.

This move increased our unpopularity, as I suppose it was bound to do, since it touched the whole Greek society at a sensitive point. The former owners took the point of view that we had spurned a generous gift. In answer to this there was nothing to be done but to pay for the slaves. I offered seven gold sovereigns for each of them. The money was taken with not very good grace.

There were some who were intellectually curious about our point of view, however. I remember in particular a man of the name of Protagoras. I gathered he was some kind of teacher, so perhaps he had a professional interest. Quite a crowd assembled when we started to argue. What none of them could understand, even the most reasonable ones, was how we got menial tasks performed in our country if we had no slaves. To the answer that we either did such tasks ourselves or paid some poorer but still free person to do them for us, they expressed frank disbelief. There was so much to be done they said, in the fields, the factories, and in the home. Surely we couldn't do it all ourselves? The argument was pressed home quite skilfully and at considerable length. The gist of their point of view was that if you didn't have slaves you'd have no leisure whatsoever. Plainly we were men of leisure. How else could I play the great lyre-in-the-box so skilfully?

There was really nothing for it except to explain that much of the manual work, which they found so necessary, was performed by machine in our society. This they couldn't understand, so I was pressed into giving descriptions and details. The bog got deeper and ever more sticky. As they took me more and more for a foolish liar I became angry. I asked them

116

if it was possible to propel a boat without sail and without oars. Of course not, they insisted.

So it came about that we made a journey to our yacht still anchored in the harbour at Piraeus. We had been in the habit of going over there two or three times a week, to make sure everything was all right, and gradually to transfer various articles of which we might have need. Lately we had managed to make the journey without too much in the way of an attendant retinue. Now however there was a huge procession as we walked the eight miles of the wall to the harbour. Quite a number of the foremost citizens turned out. There was my former host, Andocides, Cleon, the people's leader, a sculptor of the name of Myron, and an old boy who turned out to be none other than Sophocles. Everybody apparently wanted to give the lie to these boastful strangers.

I said we could manage to take half a dozen of them. Cleon and half his retinue stepped forward, setting themselves immediately above the rest. I left Alex to sort out the job of who was going to go with us. Morgan and I went out to the yacht. We spent some time working at the engine, making sure there was adequate fuel in the tank. When the motor had spluttered a few times, and was clearly on the point of starting, I signalled to the party on shore to come aboard. Nothing ever seemed to put Alex out of humour. As if it was all a big joke he somehow managed to limit the number to the specified six. Somehow he kept the others back as the six climbed aboard, the politicians I noticed.

The engine sprang to life. We soon had the anchor up. Then we were out in the bay. Morgan took the wheel and immediately made the mistake of turning north, into the straits between the island of Salamis and the mainland. As a naval officer he obviously had a fancy to see these straits, where the great Persian fleet had been defeated less than fifty years earlier. The mistake was that we were headed towards the city of Megera, an enemy city, in some ways the cause of the war itself. To those on deck it must have seemed as if we were determined to hand them over to the enemy. Only by locking ourselves in the little cabin could they be prevented from taking over the boat. We put on speed to about ten knots, which astonished the natives. There were ships in the straits.

We went quite close to them and swished past with contemptuous ease. The whole trip around the island took I suppose about five hours.

On the way back, when it was realized that we had no unpleasant intentions, the atmosphere thawed a good deal. Everybody seemed in good spirits as we made our way back to port. The crowd on shore had grown even larger. I expected something in the way of a great cheer, such as might greet a troopship coming into harbour. Instead there was a curious silence. We prepared to return to shore. This was not to be, however. The boat was invaded by determined men. They wanted to see exactly how the trick was done. What was it we had up our sleeves? Men swarmed everywhere. There was nothing for it but to show them the engines. We started them up again. We showed one group after another, in a seemingly endless sequence, the rotating propeller shaft. I think they realized how the boat came to be propelled through the water. What they couldn't understand was what was going on inside the engine.

I knew exactly what was going to happen. We should never have control of our boat again. At any rate not until they had taken it entirely to pieces. Perhaps when they couldn't put the engine together again, or if they ran out of fuel, they would call on us for help. Everybody was very pleasant and polite, but now it was they who wanted us back to shore.

We had in the cabin a transistor radio receiver and transmitter. It was obvious we should take them with us, to enable us still to contact our naval friends. Indeed we had agreed to make radio contact, since it was always possible the weather would turn out to be too bad for us to make our agreed rendezvous. So we returned to Athens carrying the radio equipment ourselves. Two days later we were told our boat had been commandeered by the city. I was not surprised. With so much speed its uses in the war would obviously be very great. All along I had realized it would be unreasonable not to expect something like this to happen. I blamed myself for not keeping my big mouth shut. In a way I had been just as foolish as Morgan.

The incident did improve our popularity however. I no longer had the feeling we might be thrown into prison at any moment. This had not been an idle fear. Only seven years earlier the great Phidias, the designer of the Parthenon itself, had died in prison.

Now within the space of a fortnight two remarkable things happened. Messengers arrived from the north. There was great excitement in the city. We thought the long awaited penetration into Greece from the Balkans had occurred. We were wrong. It was the Delphic Oracle. The prophecy was that a continuation of the war would prove the ruination of Athens, a disaster to Sparta, and to the whole of Greece. This was the meaning, it was said, of the great roaring bird which had appeared in the sky at the time of the solstice.

Nobody in Athens had ever referred to the day when we had flown directly over the city. Many tens of thousands of persons must have seen our plane. Yet not a soul had said a word about it. To mention it was to court ill-luck apparently, to tempt providence, to give substance to the portent. Now the meaning was made known. The oracle's words had far more effect than I could have expected. The discussions that went on in the Agora, in the hall of Poikile, had every aspect of rationality about them. Yet not far beneath the surface there was a deep instinctive belief in the supernatural. The old beliefs were not very far away, just as the Middle Ages were not really very far away from twentieth-century Britain.

An important effect for us personally was that our standing was enormously improved. The very reason for our previous unpopularity, Morgan's uncompromising advocacy of peace, was now the word of the oracle. Why I wondered had the oracle spoken in this fashion? None of us could recall any mention of it in classical literature.

With our new-found popularity there was a lot of music making. Alex had suddenly lost his inhibitions about playing in front of people. I guessed it might be the girl with whom he was now living, a Corinthian of great beauty, named Lais. She was taller than most of the Greek girls, fair like many of them. This was something that had surprised me, how much fairer the general population was than I'd expected. It was of course the Dorian strain which had come in from the north a century or two earlier. Anyway Alex had got himself a succulent specimen, and good luck to him, I thought. At about that time he developed a passion for Hungarian gypsy music. It proved surprisingly popular with everybody. We used to bash away at the stuff. Somehow Alex got them all whirling around like dervishes.

I played my part adequately but without real gusto. I was now seriously worried by the fact that we still heard nothing at all from the outside. It scarcely seemed credible. And there was a second queer thing.

Soon after the episode of the yacht we tried out our radio receiver. Not a sound could we get on it. Convinced the electronics had gone wrong we switched on the transmitter. Whereupon we almost blew the receiver. One afternoon I set out on a long walk. About ten miles from Athens I turned on the transmitter which I had managed to bring with me without attracting notice. On my return to Athens I found Morgan had easily picked up my transmission. Of course it was one thing to pick up a transmission from only ten miles away and quite something else to receive signals from stations a thousand miles or more away. But the transmitters back home were vastly more powerful than our little piece of equipment. It could all be explicable in terms of a lowered sensitivity of the receiver. But it could be something quite different.

The others had not been through the strange experiences of August and September in quite the way I had. Probably for this reason I was more sensitive to the situation than they appeared to be. My fear was that another gross shift had taken place. It looked to me as though the juxtaposition of different worlds and different times might have come to an end. Those different worlds might have come together for a brief spell and then separated again. It could be that we had managed to transfer ourselves from the twentieth century to the fifth century B.C., and now there was no simple retreat. It could be our naval friends would never appear off the coast of Crete, not in this world anyway. Otherwise it seemed to me quite impossible to explain our continued isolation from the outside world.

These thoughts filled my mind. I was in a stormy, gloomy mood as the time for our visit drew to an end. As it turned out the weather itself was stormy, the seas rough, and there would have been no possibility of our putting out in the small yacht. We had heard nothing further about it so presumably it was still in the hands of the shipbuilders. I was hardly worried about this aspect of the matter. Our main reason for leaving by sea had been to avoid disturbing the people here too much. If they wanted to take an awkward line that was just too bad. Now we should just have to wait until the external world arrived here, if it ever did. If there was no external world now, then there was little point in our putting to sea.

More and more as the days passed an explosion boiled up inside me. I tried to get it all out of my system, in long fierce sessions at the piano. Our house was not large and these violent sessions soon became wearying to my companions. Increasingly I thought of moving somewhere by myself, to some place where I could play to myself, not always to an audience. Another thing, I was becoming fed up with always being odd-man out. There was Morgan and Anna who made a pair, Alex and his girl friend, and myself, alone. Somehow it didn't fit.

12 Largo Appassionato

The others greeted the suggestion that I might go off for a few weeks to get some composition done with an ill-disguised enthusiasm. The question was where to go. I wanted space. In summer when it would be possible to spend much of the day outdoors these small houses would be fine. Now in winter it was altogether too cramping. Yet where was I to get space? The city was obviously overcrowded, everywhere. We started to make inquiries. The solution came in a curious way.

My stormy sessions at the piano had not passed unnoticed. There was the madness of Dionysus in it. And the dances, the gipsy music, the gay music I somehow contrived to play for our numerous visitors, was also the music of Dionysus. I was told of a temple to the god some fifteen miles down the peninsula. It was said to be in a pleasant spot overlooking the sea. Why did I not go there if I wanted to be alone? I could take two slaves, or rather two servants, to see to my needs. To the Greeks it was a logical solution.

I visited the temple. Space there certainly was. I had no quarrel with the site, only with the winds that blew there. Yet there was plenty of wood, colossal quantities of it, within easy range. It would be easier to build magnificent fires here than it was in the city. All in all the solution seemed a possible one.

The transition from the city to the temple was made smoothly and easily. I was once again amazed by the ease with which the piano was transported. The middle-aged couple came with me. It was from them, during the coming months, that I gradually acquired reasonable proficiency in the language. Isolated down the coast there was nobody else to speak to. Not that I had any overriding desire to talk but the practical matters of everyday life had to be attended to. There were the fires to be built in the right places, tables where I could write, and so on.

For now a great fever of composition was on me. I had

always composed before out of a sense of duty, really because it was my job. I had made plans of the kind of music I would write and then more or less carried them out. This time I needed no plans. The sounds simply filled my head of their own accord. What I had to do was to order them and to write them down. Only later did I realize that this was the right way. When you feel compelled to write music you write good music. The compulsion came from the experiences of the previous months. The shock and tragedy of the beginning of the whole affair. The thoughts of men who emerged from the trenches into a clean and decent world again. The landing on the great Plain of Glass with its wonderful shimmering colours. Then this delicate but deadly civilization in which I was now living. The agony, the loneliness, and the grandeur were all there in my head, above all the mystery of it. The emotions were there. Gradually the sounds built themselves to give expression to the emotions.

I worked at an ever-increasing intensity. The Greek couple were quite convinced I was mad, and in a sense I was. Never had I been so entirely gripped by the task in hand. I would go to bed utterly exhausted in the evening. Strangely enough, I had little difficulty in falling asleep. Perhaps even more strangely I wakened early, feeling quite refreshed again. Time passed almost without my realizing it. A whole symphony grew until everything was there, orchestral sketch and all. Only the more or less mechanical details of the final copy remained. While the fever was on me there was no point at all in taking up time in a straightforward job. So I rushed on to other ideas, which were now forming. Two sonatas simply tumbled out, more properly sonata-fantasias. The urge to break the bounds of all the forms proved irresistible. The symphony had structure but it wasn't a structure I could put a name to.

Then I began the work that was to consume me for over two months. It was for orchestra and chorus. I fretted and fumed for a while. I had no literature. I wanted words to give expression to the kind of feeling I now had within me. I had thrashed around for several days before the obvious solution occurred to me, first to conceive the music and its moods, then to write appropriate words myself. It was the species of work all composers want to write, what in the old days would have taken the form of a Mass, set to the standard text. My lack of belief in the text, the usual Credo for instance, would have made a mockery of a formal Mass.

By this new method I was entirely free to build the musical structure as I went along. I was not inhibited by the need to set meaningless words. It was the creation, the meaning, the purpose of the world that had significance. It was the tragedy of man, the tragedy that he can sense such problems but not solve them, which overwhelmed me. The last thing I wanted was easy solutions beginning with the words 'I believe'. It was the juxtaposition in all of us of the primitive with something better that troubled me.

Early on, my friends and the people of Athens came out to see me quite often. I was so ill-mannered at these interruptions that the visits became less and less frequent. By the time of the first spring flowers I had become almost a hermit. Even Alex hardly came any more. Only in retrospect did I realize this for at the time I was entirely preoccupied. Undoubtedly in the popular mind I was now well-placed, a mad priest in the temple of Dionysus. Gradually the work came to an end, the fires began to damp themselves down. I looked around me and realized where I was. I began to think again about the everyday world. There seemed no doubt now but that my wild prognostication was correct. The different ages of the Earth which had come momentarily together had somehow separated again. Otherwise there would have been evidence long ago of the vibrant, harsh civilization of Europe.

As the spring days lengthened I became more and more fretful. Once again I had the need of human company. I decided the time had come for a return to the city. One day I made the journey alone. After the quietness of the winter the noise of the city startled my ears. I came at last to my friends' house. For a moment I had the irrational fear that they too would be gone leaving me alone in a new existence. But there they were, heartily glad to see me apparently safe and well.

I was all agog to hear the news:

'Have you heard anything at all from our people?'

'Not a thing,' answered Morgan.

From his face I could see that at last he too was worried. 'What does it mean? Man, they must have been here before now. How is it that nobody comes?'

'We'd better face it I think. Somehow this world, this time, has cut adrift again. I don't know how. I don't know how it happened before, how they ever came together. But we're adrift now, that's the only way it can be.'

Alex was the least perturbed of the three of them, he still had his girl friend apparently. Anna began to weep, almost silently. Morgan went over to comfort her as best he could. Then he came back to me:

'What's to be done? We've just got to decide on some course of action.'

'How about the boat? Have they said anything about it?'

'I gather they've loused it up. The engine I mean. Still we might put it in shape again, if we're lucky.'

'Maybe we should go into the prophecy business. We ought to do pretty well in that line.'

We chatted on for several hours. I decided I was moving back to the house. It would really have been more sensible to have spent the winter in the city, then to have gone out into the country now in the spring. But this would be to order one's life by rational argument. The period I had just come through was not the sort of thing one could legislate for. We began to discuss details. The best thing would be to move back in two or three weeks' time. There was still quite a bit of work to be done. It was more or less plain sailing now. But I would get through the scoring quicker by myself than in the middle of an uproar. With this settled I returned to the temple.

When I came to the reasonably straightforward parts of my work I became restless. I found it impossible to devote the same long hours, ten hours or more each day. I found it best to put in five or six hours in the morning, to take a long walk in the afternoon, and so early to bed. I came to move more and more about the peninsula. Not that I could yet go very far. I began looking forward to the prospect of longer trips. I decided that in April and May I would make a journey into the Pelopponesus, if circumstances permitted it.

One day I came on a large temple on the slopes of the mountain of Aegaleos. This was the hill from which Xerxes was said to have watched the defeat of his fleet at Salamis. The temple was to Apollo. It stood on a flat grassy knoll covered with a profusion of wild flowers set in a beautiful meadow. After winter in my rougher accommodation down by the sea it seemed just about perfect. The day was almost unaccountably soft up here. I remembered the strange oracle from Delphi. That too came from the temple of Apollo. From the god himself according to the beliefs of these people.

The immediate approaches to the temple were carefully kept. I walked up the steps out of the sun into the darkened interior. At the far end there was a door, or rather an opening, into an enclosed garden. Flowers were to be seen everywhere in the garden. I was looking generally around when I heard a quiet sound behind me. I turned quickly to find a girl looking down at me from the top of a short flight of steps. She was instantly different from any girl I had yet seen. The hair was of the usual light brown, but the eyes were grey. At first I thought she seemed tall because she had the advantage of the steps. Then I realized that indeed she was tall, of almost my own height.

'This is a beautiful day on which to meet a beautiful girl in such a garden as this.'

My Greek was still not very fluent, but I hoped it would be good enough.

'Not many come here. You are welcome.'

I found this difficult to believe, with such a girl as this. Yet possibly she was too tall to be attractive to the average Greek male.

'I fear I came without any knowledge that you would be here. So I brought nothing to sacrifice to the god, or even a small gift to please you.'

'I see from your face you are a stranger.'

'It would be a lucky man on whom you would look with favour.'

The girl threw back her head and laughed. Then she became serious and said, 'You forget where you are. We are not now in the temple of Dionysus.'

There was nothing unfavourable in this. By now I knew enough of Greek customs to realize what was meant, or at least I thought so. Two advances, two retreats, then a decision. Enough dalliance to satisfy the human sense of dignity, not so much as to be an undue waste of time. The enormous death rate from disease and war demanded a high birth rate. I felt I knew exactly where I stood. I took the girl's hand in mine, prepared to make a pretty speech, when to my surprise she said:

126

'What you would have must be worked for. I must remind you again what place this is.'

Of course she meant she was a priestess of Apollo. Yet I was unaware of anything inhibiting about such an occupation. Perhaps the time of the year was wrong.

'All worthwhile things must be earned. It will be my pleasure to do whatever you wish.'

'Are you not the strange man who for months past has sacrificed himself to Dionysus?'

I was a bit sensitive to this suggestion. Just because I had been forced to use the temple down by the shore, to avoid living in a rabbit hutch, was no reason why I should be thought insane. Yet I had some idea of what the girl meant. I had been puzzled in the beginning by the attitude of the Greeks to their gods. On the face of it religion did not seem to be taken very seriously. But in at least one important respect the gods were still thought of in terms of reality. The gods represented a quintessence of human emotions and abilities. Madness, wild actions, lack of restraint, moderated by genuine spontaneity, those were the qualities of Dionysus, the qualities I appeared to possess. In a way the judgement was fair enough. Here in the temple of Apollo the idea was of controlled form, aesthetics in general. This was the place where beauty did not need to be sensual.

'You practice your art without licence. *This* is the abode of music.'

Now I saw what she was driving at. Apollo of course was the god of song and music. By not making obeisances in the temple of the god I had in effect set myself up in opposition to him. I was guilty of sacrilege, at any rate in the eyes of his priestess. If I hoped to make any further progress with her it would plainly be necessary to carry out some act of appeasement. A further assessment of the situation persuaded me appeasement would be worthwhile provided it was not too serious. I was wondering just what to suggest when she said:

'You will remember what happened to the satyr Marsyas?'

I racked my brains as to who this satyr fellow might be. Clearly I was being compared to him, not flatteringly I suspected. Then it flashed through my mind that the fellow was supposed to have engaged Apollo in a musical contest, the one on the lyre, the other on the flute. I had a notion he came to a sticky end.

'I would be ready to engage in any contest that seemed fitting.'

'You are haunted by a foolish pride.'

I could not help smiling for the thought of a contest between a primitive lyre and a modern piano seemed ludicrous.

'You cannot really mean such a contest is possible?' I asked in frank incredulity.

For answer the girl took me into the temple. She showed me a lyre measuring about a yard across. She played a melody on it. The inference was obvious. The girl, or some other person in the temple, was indeed willing to engage in a musical trial of strength.

'It will be necessary for me to fetch my own instrument.'

'That was expected. You will come two days before the next full moon. You may bring what you please and you may bring whom you please. We shall begin half-way through the last third of the day.'

We walked amicably out of the front entrance of the temple. We strolled through the field to the beginning of the pathway down the mountain. There were still one or two points to be settled:

'Who is to be the judge?'

'We shall be the judges, you and I.'

'And the stake? What is the winner to receive and what the loser?'

'You have already made your request clear. What the penalty might be I will leave you to reflect upon during the coming days.'

I started down the path in excellent spirits. My only worry in such a contest would have been the judges. Anything might happen if untrained ears were permitted a vote. This way, with the girl and myself as judges, the worst that could happen would be a stalemate.

I sat down at the piano to recover the melody the girl had played. It was a beautiful thing, a little sad, but a great deal better than anything I had yet heard since coming to Greece. Someone at the temple, if not the girl herself, was very much out of the common run. I supposed they were aware of it. No doubt this was why the challenge had been issued. I began to play variations on the melody. It was certainly a beautiful thing but no better than hundreds of other melodies that could be conjured up. With the whole of European musical literature behind me there could be no question of the outcome of the contest.

I walked into Athens the following morning. My story put Alex Hamilton once again into fits of laughter. 'Wonderful, that's quite marvellous.'

Of course everybody soon knew about it, Alex saw to that. To him it was the joke of the year. I was not surprised to find the Greeks taking it more seriously. One or two of them, particularly I remember a chap of the name of Diagoras, came and congratulated me. They said it was high time the old superstitions were broken. From the gravity of their manner, I realized the superstitions went deeper than even they themselves supposed.

I suspect I would soon have had an ugly situation on my hands if the people hadn't felt the god to be entirely capable of looking after himself. It was as though I had desecrated a temple, not a trivial offence.

My worry that too many people would flock on to the hill was apparently shared also by the Boule, the council of the city. A decree was quickly passed that nobody outside my personal party was to approach the temple within ten stadia, that is to say within a mile.

Only on the morning of the day itself did the full implication of the situation really become clear to me. The way I had fixed things with the priestess this was to be a private affair. There was no suggestion of a public contest. In fact that had been exactly my worry. I wanted to avoid a contest by popular acclamation. Yet in a sense this was exactly what it had become. Even worse, how could I possibly win? Even if the priestess were to come down on my side she could hardly say so in public. The populace would tear her limb from limb. And the stalemate, which I had fondly imagined would be the worst that could befall me, would become a mockery if those at the temple should declare against me. I saw I was in really serious trouble. I also saw the priestess had probably planned this from the beginning. My crime against the god was probably a serious one in her eyes. I started up the pathway in the middle morning with far less enthusiasm than I had come down it four days before.

My forebodings proved very accurate. Even in the early afternoon a considerable crowd was already gathered on the flat ground in front of the temple. They obeyed the orders of the city fathers up to a point. They were keeping about three hundred yards from the temple. I had no doubt the city fathers themselves would come even closer. I was accosted by a small, ugly-looking man:

'Is it really true you are to engage the god in a contest?'

'Is it really true there is a god?'

'I see it is true.'

He looked me over for a long time. Then reflectively he added, 'Well, well, it should prove interesting.'

I looked him over carefully. 'Can I ask you a question? Are you sure of anything?'

'I am sure the summer is hot and the winter cold.'

'And you are sure your fellow citizens have too many preconceived opinions?'

'Of that I am also sure. They say the last one to challenge the god was flayed alive for his pains. Of that I am *not* sure.'

'Thank you for your encouragement.'

I left him at the foot of the temple steps. I had reached the top, when as an afterthought I shouted, 'By the way, have you paid that cock to Asclepius yet?'

Nuts, I thought, as I walked into the temple. This just can't be true. But the stone pillars were hard enough and the piano was real enough. It was a meeting of two different worlds.

By now I had some experience of the best place to site the piano in order to get the best resonant effects. The men who carried it up knew nothing of this so it had to be moved. I had to go out again to get the necessary help. Once I was satisfied with the position, my helpers cleared off just as quickly as they could.

I still had a long tuning job. I wanted to make the best possible job for the acoustics in the temple were wonderful.

Already we were in the third part of the day, the third division of the day, so I wouldn't have much longer to wait. I strolled outside and came on Alex, Morgan, Anna, and a few Greek friends who were still willing to stand by me.

Alex was somewhat contrite at the commotion he had

caused. 'Don't worry, just play,' he said. 'You can't lose, except by being too ambitious.'

I suggested it would be best if they came through the temple to the little inner garden. The piano was placed towards that end and they would hear better from there.

'I think it's going to be a good evening,' said Anna. This might well be true. The remarkable carrying power of sound was one of the secrets of the Greek open air theatre. On many evenings the sound travelled horizontally instead of upwards, as it tends to do in northern climates.

The light inside the temple was not very good. It was fortunate I had decided to trust my memory. As the light gradually faded it would have been difficult to read notes inside here. Actually I had no fears upon the musical side, the troubles were political. I guessed the whole thing was a trick organized by the politicians we had offended soon after our arrival.

So far nobody from the other side had shown themselves in the temple. Now at last a priest appeared. He was of a similar colouring to the girl priestess, light brown hair, and he was similarly tall. In the subdued light I could not judge the colour of his eyes.

'Is it your wish to proceed with the contest?'

I suppose in the circumstances it would have been sensible for me to have called it all off. There was no point in running my head into a political noose. Yet this was ostensibly a musical contest. How could I retreat from a trial of strength in my own craft? Perhaps it was pride which impelled me to go on but I think not.

'Yes, I wish to continue.'

The priest then withdrew. Some five minutes later the first sounds came. I say came because I had no idea as to their exact source. It had to be from one or other of the three side chambers opening out from the main floor.

The melody was the one the girl had played for me four days earlier. The melody was the same but the instrument was not. It had a far clearer, more penetrating, quality. It was played with much greater decision. If this indeed was the girl then she had been fooling me before. The melody was followed by a complex variation from which it emerged again as a single line. But now the line was changed, in a fashion I couldn't exactly determine. There were three more variations, each rapidly and lightly played. Following each one came the melody, always with changes. It was as if the tune were made to evolve through the intervening sections of complex structure. This was all I could make out in the beginning. It lasted for some six or seven minutes.

Now it was my turn. I decided to match the light rippling music I had just heard. I think it was Liszt who referred to shooting the octaves out of one's shirt-sleeves. I played four Chopin studies. This I felt was a fair return. Even though I had kept things very light and delicate it was clear the piano was more wonderful than whatever instrument was being played behind the scenes. Even so I was amazed at the quality of what I had heard. It was really beautiful miniature stuff, enormously superior to anything I had heard in the city. Who the hell was playing it I began to wonder.

The next round was instantly more serious. The texture was fuller and louder. Yet the precision of detail was still there. A casual listener would have judged there to be long and short notes, exactly as in our own music. Yet this was not so. Every note was short. The impression of a long note was given by several short notes played very close together. You can't do this at all on a piano, no matter how quickly you move your finger. It takes the key so long to respond that by the time you press it for a second time the total volume generated by the first note has already fallen so far that the second one stands out as a quite separate pulse of sound. In this case, when a long note was desired the second pulse came before the first one had died more than a little way. There was a slight dying effect of course, otherwise the note would have been long and uniform, exactly the way it can be on a violin. Here you could just about detect the separation of the pulses. This indeed was one of the things which gave the music its quite novel sound. It was as if somebody were plucking a string at an enormously high rate, as if the string were responding instantly. So much could I make out of the individual notes themselves.

It still baffled me as to exactly what restrictions were being placed on the choice of the notes themselves. This was not twelve-tone music, all the tones were not being used. Yet it wasn't tonal in the sense of our system of keys. The structure was more complicated than anything I had heard before. I had the strong impression of rules depending somehow on the form of the work itself. It was as if the rules, the restrictions, depended on the place in the piece. The rules at the beginning and those at the end seemed different, and different again from those in the middle. It was as if the large-scale development of the work influenced its manner of construction.

I mention all this to show why it wasn't in any way easy even for a trained musician to grasp instantly what was going on. Plainly I had to deal with a subtle and complex form. My last thought of the people outside was that they could hardly find the music of the god easier to comprehend than my own. I think it was at this point, as the second of my opponent's sections came to an end, that the first chill of apprehension swept over me.

My response was essentially automatic. I made my choices from *The Art of Fugue*. I made them instinctively, allowing the music to well out of the fingertips. As I came to an end I no longer had any idea of playing to the crowd outside, or even to my friends in the little garden, but to whatever it was that lay out of sight somewhere in the darkening temple.

With the beginning of the third trial all was changed. The music was now full-toned, slow and majestic. Its quality and power was a fitting tribute to the gods. This was no simple priest or priestess, or even a thousand of them. A power was abroad here that could not be denied. It was a power hitting at me, not at the crowd. There was no appeal to popular taste, even the popular taste of the twentieth century. It was exactly what it claimed to be, Apollonian in stature.

Although I was far more concerned to listen now than to analyse, I was overwhelmingly impressed by the tonal ambivalence, by the difficulty of deciding what note or chord would come next. Even before the end was reached I knew there could only be one answer.

I began the Adagio Sostenuto from Beethoven's Opus 106. I took the tempo as slow as I dared. The movement, long as it is, had now to be stretched to the limit. The sonority was wonderful, every note rang out true and clear. The minutes passed and the music flowed everlastingly on. It might be the god himself who was opposing me, yet he should learn something of the depths of human agony. I was already playing the arpeggiated bass chords that bring the movement to an end when the fantastic risk I had taken flashed through my mind. But the memory I had always relied on so heavily in the past had not let me down. Nor could I have ever been reconciled to myself if it had.

There came a long pause. It did not signify the end, I knew. A pause was necessary for aesthetic reasons. I was sitting waiting when a light step caused me to swivel suddenly and apprehensively round. It was the girl, the priestess, dressed in a quite beautiful long gown. It had no relation to the dresses of the women of Athens. It buttoned around the neck in a manner reminding me of the costume of a Chinese woman.

'It is necessary for the last part that you should play only the music you have written yourself.'

After this calm command she was gone.

So the ground was swept from under me as the first notes of my opponent's last section rang out loud and triumphantly. It was altogether bigger in its proportion than the previous rounds. It was quite symphonic in scale, although there was no suggestion of orchestral instruments. Everything was built out of plucked notes. It lacked something of the colour of an orchestra but this can be my only criticism. How much of it I failed to appreciate with my ears untrained to the basic style I do not know. Yet enough of the splendour of it was clear to me for the near hopelessness of my position to be obvious. Yet it was only at the end that desperation seized me. While the music played I listened with bowed head.

I knew I could only answer one vision of creation with another. I needed full orchestra and chorus, all I had was a single piano. I sat for a little while, the sweat dripping down my face. Then I began with the slow maestoso section of my last work. A lifetime's discipline of listening to what I was playing steadied my nerves. The ideas came back more and more. Gradually the intense fury of those winter months re-asserted itself. How long I played I could not tell. It was quite dark now, apart from shafts of moonlight coming through the entrances to the temple. I came at last to a convenient stopping point. Then I just sat, silently waiting.

The girl came to me. Without seeing any clear-cut gesture I realized she wanted me to follow her. I kept two or three paces behind as we crossed the main floor. We came out of a side entrance into the open moonlight. The scent of flowers seemed overwhelmingly strong.

'You may sit here if you wish,' almost in a whisper.

I sat down, not because I was tired, but because it was the easiest way to unwind myself.

'What is your verdict?' she asked.

So they were sticking to the bargain, whoever they were.

'I can say nothing about the end, my last piece. You asked for it to be my own. Nobody can give a fair judgement of his own music. Of the other three parts, I do not think I lost.'

'Do you wish to claim victory, even apart from the fourth and last section?'

I thought for a long time. All my instinct told me that nothing could equal Bach or the finest of Beethoven. Yet the mere fact I hesitated showed it would be wrong to claim too much. I knew the works of Bach and Beethoven as I knew the back of my own hand, so I was familiar with their tremendous merits. I had heard this new music but once. It was inconceivable I could have distilled out of a single hearing all that was in it.

'No, I do not wish to claim victory. But you, what is your opinion?' I asked.

In a soft voice, the girl replied, 'I am content to take the same view.'

The load lifted instantly from my mind. It was the proper verdict. The styles were too different for a judgement of better or worse to be made. Only similar things can be compared in a direct fashion, only when they set out to obey the same rules and restrictions.

'So we end as we began. Except I hope you will no longer think of me as an uncontrolled madman.'

'I never did, I simply wanted to hear you play.'

The cool effrontery of this reply shattered my growing complacency. The girl went on. 'Because you make no claims for your own work, I will give you that which you asked for.'

She took me a few steps further into the little side garden, to where I could see a flat couch. I was rather surprised she paid no heed to the crowds outside. I suppose she thought the people would be so frightened at what they had heard that there could be no danger of them entering the temple. She laughed quite openly as I began to kiss her.

The night was a subtle compound of many ingredients.

Moments of high passion, of whispered conversation and laughter bubbling along like a stream in the woods, of the scent of the flowers, of snatches of sleep, and of long intervals lying quiet – the girl in my arms – looking up at the sky above our heads. Time was measured not on my watch but by the changing positions of the stars. It was not until the glow of morning was spreading upward from the eastern horizon that at last I fell into a deep sleep.

I awoke with the instant conviction of having slept long and wonderfully well. With languorous disappointment I realized the girl had gone. It was not until I heaved myself into a sitting posture that the first shock came. I was inside some building. It was obviously not the temple. For a flash I thought I had been carried away to prison. Then I saw this could be no prison, it was far too comfortable.

Not only that but I was dressed in a queer garment. It could be said to be a pair of pyjamas, or more accurately pyjamas, because as far as I could see I was completely fastened up in the damn thing. It was all in one piece and there seemed to be no possibility of getting it either on or off. The material too was strange. It was coloured in a multitudinous and expensive manner. It somehow suggested Joseph's coat, yet the colours were delicate rather than garish.

Quickly I jumped out of bed. Then I saw it wasn't a bed. It was simply a flat piece of the floor of the room itself, but raised two or three feet above the rest of the floor. The carpeting, or whatever it was, was extremely soft to the tread. I didn't bother to examine it but moved quickly to the opening out of the room – there was no door. I came into a very large room indeed, a room which was odd in the extreme. To begin with, there wasn't a single chair, not a single item of furniture, in the usual sense. The floor was in the same deep blue material as the bedroom. It was everywhere uneven. It had raised and lowered portions in no particular pattern that I could discern. The walls and the ceiling were coloured in a fashion both gay and restrained. The dominant colours were different on the different walls, one had green and yellows, another was tinged largely with gold, another red. The overall shape was rectangular. Generally speaking the walls were vertical. Like the floor, however, there were few strictly plain surfaces. The effect was pleasing and soothing. One side of the room was open, and I could see sunshine beyond a curtaining material. I tried to get through the curtain but I could find no means of pulling the material aside. It took some minutes before I got the trick of it. I noticed that one could simply put one's hand through it, as if the whole fabric were rotten. Then I walked through it. Instead of the tear being permanent the material closed up behind me.

I was out on a large balcony. The house was built on the side of a hill. A smooth path came towards it from a near-by clump of trees. This was the only sign of a road I could see anywhere. Apart from the hum of insects it was quite silent. Everywhere over the hillside, running for miles in all directions, were banks of flowers and trees. I saw an occasional glimpse of some other house. Below me in the distance lay green fields. In the very far distance the mountains rising high into the sky were snow capped.

13 Allegretto e Sempre Cantabile

My first thought was that I had awakened at last from a long nightmare, or more likely from some fever. It was in Hawaii everything had started to go wrong. At a first glance here I was back again in Hawaii. The quality of the light, the high mountains, were superficially similar. Could this strange building be some kind of isolation hospital?

The pyjamas I was wearing might also at first glance have been taken for some exotic Hawaiian garment. But the material wasn't right, it was much too expensive in its weave and colouring. Then nobody I had ever known had conceived of a house like this, not even in the wildest dreams. Besides it couldn't be Hawaii. Those mountains must be at least fifty miles away. The visibility was tremendous. At such a range on Hawaii I would have been looking out over the sea but there was no sign of an ocean. There had been many flowers on Hawaii but nothing to compare with this luxuriant profusion.

Step by step I went over recent events. The night at the temple was last night. I was convinced of it. Yet this was quite certainly not Greece. The style of the house, its spaciousness, the countryside, and above all those mountains, were definitely not Grecian.

Although strange and singular things had been happening, up to this point they had not happened to me personally. This was the first big jump in my own personal consciousness. Subjectively I felt quite normal, yet objectively it seemed as if I must be as nutty as a squirrel.

I decided to search the house. I saw a second curtain opening off the balcony. As it was of the same material as before I simply walked through it without experiencing any sensation except a gentle brushing against the cheek. There were further rooms, smaller but designed in much the same fashion as the big room. However in one of them there was a table. It was the only article of furniture to be seen anywhere.

On it was a considerable pile of musical manuscripts. The briefest inspection showed they were the works on which I had spent the winter, in the little temple of Dionysus. At least in that respect I was not crazy. I flicked through the pages. My memory was right in every respect, all the details were in place, exactly as they should have been. At least some things were right, inexplicable as the basic facts seemed on the face of it. I went back to the large room. Sitting there on the floor was John Sinclair.

I collapsed by his side and said weakly, 'What the hell's going on?'

'I thought you might be getting worried. I've been round twice before but you were asleep. It's incredible you managed to get here.'

'Incredible?'

'You'd better tell me exactly what happened, before you woke up to find yourself here I mean.'

I started to give a general outline of my experience in Greece. John would have none of it. He demanded I should go through everything in complete detail. I came at last to the night in the temple. At the end of my description of the contest with the god, John began to laugh delightedly.

Remembering the ordeal I said, sourly, 'You're not the only one to find it funny. By now the whole of Athens will be laughing hysterically about it.'

'Piqued, eh? You know it's ironical. While I would have been quite incapable myself of putting up any sort of musical performance, I could have told you straightaway what it was you were dealing with.'

'What the devil d'you mean?'

'Isn't it perfectly obvious? It was the music of the future.'

I sat digesting this as best I could. He went on, 'Perhaps now you can realize why I was so keen to look everywhere, all over the Earth. Don't think I didn't want to come with you to Greece. I would have loved it, but I was convinced that the Britain of 1966 wasn't the last moment of time to be abroad on the Earth. Remember all the different periods we saw, perhaps five thousand B.C. in the Middle East, four hundred B.C. in Greece, the eighteenth century in America, 1917 in Europe, why stop at 1966 in Britain? There had to be something more.'

'So you went on searching?'

'High and low. We drew a complete blank everywhere in the southern hemisphere. I can't be entirely sure about South America because we ran into terrible weather there. You remember the Plain of Glass?'

I nodded and he went on:

'You see that just had to be the distant future, far away in the future.'

'Why?'

John made no immediate answer. He took a small box-like device from his pocket and pressed what seemed to be a switch. Instantly the floor became everywhere very soft, as if one had sunk into a feather bed. Because of the rises and hollows it was easy to get oneself into a comfortable position. Then he did something again to the box and the floor went quite hard again, at least hard compared to what it had been a moment before. I found myself sitting in what might have been taken for an extremely comfortable chair.

'So that's why they don't need any chairs?'

'That's right. Would you like some food?'

Now he came to mention it, I was damned hungry. I said so.

'Come on then. I'll show you some other gadgets.'

He led the way to one of the subsidiary rooms. He pressed a small button. Instantly a panel slid by and what seemed to be a typewriter keyboard appeared on one of the walls.

'What would you like?'

I said I would like fruit juice and bacon and egg.

'I'll do the best I can.'

John tapped the keyboard as if he was writing a message, then gave one final flourish, pressing what seemed to be a master button. About ten seconds later a kind of hatchway opened and out came a metal arm on which were two trays. On each tray was a large glass of yellow juice, which I took to be orange juice. There was also what seemed to be a slice of bread or toast covered in some reddish fluffy stuff.

'What the hell is this?'

'Your bacon and egg. I think I got it right.'

He dipped his finger into the froth and tasted it. Then he nodded and said, more seriously:

'Let's go back and talk.'

Somewhat bemused, I followed him. We took up our respective positions on the floor.

John explained: 'You see these people don't eat animals, so all the food is either vegetable or synthetic. There are literally hundreds of these preparations. I haven't sampled more than a small fraction of them yet.'

I tried the orange juice. It was excellent, in fact I couldn't recall tasting any better. Then I addressed myself to the froth. I had no complaint about that either. It wasn't bacon and egg by any means but it fell into the right kind of savoury class. 'Where the devil does the taste come from?'

'Well of course it's artificial in the sense the chemicals are produced synthetically, but they're the right chemicals, the ones you really get in the sort of food we're used to. Incidentally, you'll find the calorific value is quite low. You can eat bags of this stuff without growing fat.'

And then we were back to more gadgets. John had a piece of his bread and froth left. He smeared the froth on to the carpet material and chucked the piece of bread to the far side of the room. 'Time to get the sweeper out,' he remarked cheerfully. 'Better come over to the doorway.'

He took out his little box and fiddled again with it. There was a sort of blowing noise from the sides of the room, from what would be the wainscoting in a normal house. A white strip started at one side. It moved slowly across to the other side, where it finally disappeared. In its wake there was nothing but clean carpet. The whole process took about thirty seconds. John was like a boy with a toy. 'Not much trouble about housekeeping, is there?'

He stopped clowning and we went on to the balcony. He produced what looked rather like two deck chairs. Thank god for a touch of normality, I thought.

'You were talking about the Plain of Glass. Why does it belong so obviously to the future?'

'Because it's been melted, everywhere, smoothly. You know the Sun is going to get hotter and hotter as time goes on. There'll be a stage when the whole surface of the Earth melts. After that the Sun will cool. Everywhere over the Earth there'll be smooth glass. You remember what I said about it's not being etched by blown grit or sand. There couldn't be any sand with everything fused. Besides at that stage there would be no atmosphere, no wind. The Plain of Glass is the ultimate fate of the Earth.'

I sat for some time sipping my orange juice, letting all this sink in.

John went on. 'You see, it was a fair bet that if the distant future were represented here, there ought to be something in between, between 1966 and the far-off future. That's why I was so convinced it was worth going on searching.'

'Didn't you expect these people of the future would show themselves?'

'Not necessarily. Remember your own point of view about the Greeks. You were worried at the mere idea of mobs of our own people streaming into Greece. You wanted to leave it as much the way it was as you could. The future could be quite shy of appearing among us for exactly the same reason. They couldn't simply declare themselves as strangers, in the way you could when you arrived at Athens. The same thing in London would be impossible.'

'Yet they must have appeared in Greece.'

'For exactly the reason I've just given you. One thing I don't quite understand is how they've managed to keep Europeans out of Greece. You must have been lucky enough to get through their barrier before they closed it.'

'You think that's why our own people never arrived?'

'Fairly obvious, isn't it? Somehow the communication lines must have been cut. I can't quite see how, but we must realize these people are at least as far ahead of us technologically as we are ahead of the Greeks. I don't think there's much profit in worrying too much about practical details. If the Britain of 1966 could put an instant stop to the war in Europe, with only a technological lead of fifty years, a society with a lead of thousands of years wouldn't have too much trouble in hiving off a bit of the Earth. In any case that's exactly what they've done with their own country.'

I looked away towards the mountains. 'Where are we? I was trying to puzzle it out before you came. The nearest I could get was Hawaii, but that didn't seem right.'

John looked at his watch. 'It's not very far from midday. If you were to sit here for several hours you'd see the Sun move from left to right. Now work it out for yourself.'

The Sun moved from left to right, did it? I thought for a few minutes. This must mean we were in the northern hemisphere, because the Sun had to be south of the zenith. As far as

I could judge, there was an angle of about twenty degrees between the direction of the Sun and the vertical. So far so good. Then it was early spring, at least it had been only the beginning of April in Greece. If it was the same here it meant the angle between the Sun and the vertical was pretty well the geographical latitude, evidently twenty degrees north or thereabouts. My next thought was of the Himalayas. Could these mountains be the Himalayas? Then I remembered the Himalayan range is much further north than one usually supposes. In fact the equator goes south of the whole of India, the mountains come at thirty degrees north. I looked up again towards the Sun, the angle couldn't be as much as thirty degrees. Mentally I ran along a parallel of latitude, first into Burma. Obviously Burma wasn't right either, unless the vegetation was completely changed. Then I thought about Arabia and Africa. None of it fitted. The solution came to me last of all. The twentieth parallel must cut through America somewhere about Mexico City. The clarity of the air, the feeling I had of altitude, the mountains, were right.

'Mexico, of course.'

'Very good.'

'How did you get here yourself?'

'A good question, considering the way *you* got here. Damn it, I know what I'm looking for and I have to comb the whole Earth before I find it. All you have to do is to walk up a hill to a temple and what happens, you run slap bang into these people of the future.'

I had a clear memory of the priestess standing on the steps looking down at me in the little garden. So that was the explanation of why she seemed so different, why she was so tall. Melea, she had told me her name was last night, if it was last night.

'You know, John, my manuscripts. When I came up to the temple I didn't bring them with me. I left them back at the place where I was working. Somehow they must have been retrieved.'

'Oh, I'm sure you're definitely *persona grata*. After your musical performance. You see it's very likely they've lost all of our music. It must have come as quite a shock to them to hear it. I'm all right myself now, but it wasn't easy in the beginning. We got here during a storm. Otherwise I'm sure they would have misled us through the radio. We found a place to land and came down.'

'What happened to the rest of the crew?'

'I'll tell you about them in a moment. Of course the people here wanted to know who we were, all manner of detail.'

'How about language difficulties?'

'You'll see how they cope with that, all in good time.'

'So you got to the place where you wanted to be?'

'I was agog to find out what they knew. I was curious about a lot of technical problems in physics, obviously. It was like doing a puzzle in a newspaper. You're told the solution is on page eight, column four. If you find you can't do the puzzle, the natural thing is to look at the answer, which was the way I felt about a lot of things. I asked a lot of questions in return, which was lucky for me, otherwise they'd have dealt with me the same way they did with the rest of the crew.

'We had to go back in their textbooks quite a fair way before we reached the things I know about. One of my own discoveries I found under somebody else's name. Naturally I didn't take at all kindly to this. When I pointed it out, they instantly changed their tune and became very friendly. All doors were opened to me as it were. Well, two or three days after our landing, I learnt the plane was being sent away. I didn't want to go myself for obvious reasons but I did want to send a message. So I sought out the crew.'

John stopped at this point, his usual habit, just when he had reached the decisive point.

'Well,' I grunted.

'They didn't know me, they damned well didn't know me from Adam. There was nothing wrong with them physically. Of course when they made no move to recognize me it was clear the people here didn't want any message sent. I saw it wasn't a good idea to press the point. So I simply let the plane go.'

'Why didn't they recognize you?'

'Well, it's perhaps not really so surprising. What we can do with drugs, anaesthetics and so on, would seem astonishing to the Greeks, wouldn't it? I don't think they had been harmed in any way, except they would lose their memory of the whole incident. It would be a kind of artificially induced amnesia.'

144

'You think that's why I remember absolutely nothing between the temple and here?'

'I would say so. Probably they didn't want you making a fuss.'

I decided I would have another glass of orange juice. For some reason I was extremely thirsty. John gave me a description of which button to press and I went to the kitchen alone. With a bit of fiddling I got what I wanted, but I got plenty of other stuff as well. I took the whole lot back to the balcony, for I was getting hungry again. I had in fact lost weight during the winter. For the most part I had lived on fish and on a kind of cake made out of honey and flour. After such a pleasant but monotonous diet, the profusion of tastes coming from the machines in the kitchen had quite a fascination.

'How advanced are these people, technologically I mean?' I asked as I munched the odd concoctions.

'Considering they're something like six thousand years beyond us, not as much as I would have expected. At the development pace of the nineteenth and twentieth centuries, I'd say they're about five hundred years on. Of course that's impressive enough. It's about the gap which separated us from the fifteenth century. They've apparently been able to put into practice things we could only just conceive of. For instance they can produce enormous captive magnetic fields. You do this with a superconducting material, which prevents you from having ridiculous heating problems. Our trouble was that we couldn't get sufficiently rigid materials, and we had to fuss with very low temperatures. Somehow they've got rigid serviceable materials. Very strong magnetic fields have become a standard part of their technology, like the electric motor and dynamo are with us. You'll find their vehicles look at first sight like a hovercraft. They float over the ground. But they don't do it by blowing air. They simply ride on a magnetic field. The logistics of it work just like a railway system. They've got tracks laid out all over the country. But the tracks are magnetic, nothing at all like railway lines. The great thing about it is that it's all silent, and it's all computer controlled. Apparently you ring up for a vehicle in the same way as we might ring up for a taxi.'

'But with travelling as individual as that, like taxis, I'd have thought there'd be an almost impossible crush.'

'I think the secret of it is that there just aren't many people. We think in terms of tens or hundreds of millions. I haven't found out yet exactly how many of them there are, but it can't be anything like a twentieth-century population.'

It was all very intriguing. Already I had a fancy to do a bit of travelling around myself.

'How did you know to come up here?'

'I had information you were here.'

'You realize what that means?'

'I don't think it's as bad as you think. Look, who were your special friends in Greece? You give me an answer because I've asked an entirely reasonable question, not because I force an answer out of you. That's probably what you did. There may be nothing more to it.'

'And I've since forgotten all about it?'

'I thought we agreed about that. Anyway they told me you would be here. Something more, they're going to put on a special film show for us. To give us an idea of the things that have happened in the span of time between our day and theirs. I gather it'll last for quite a time, although they apologized for the sparsity of some of the material. They said we would realize why when we'd seen it.'

We went back inside to the main room. John hunted around until he found a master switch. When he pressed it the same thing happened as in the kitchen, a panel slid back and a kind of typewriter keyboard appeared. Only this time there were many more keys on it. John took out a piece of paper:

'I've got the code here, at least I've got instructions about which buttons to press. Until we get used to it we'd better do what they tell us. Otherwise we may find ourselves inside the washing machine.'

He pressed I suppose about half a dozen keys. On one of the flat pieces of the wall there appeared a picture. It was a pleasant country scene in colour, no more. 'That must be the call signal.'

We made ourselves a couple of comfortable armchairs in the floor and sat down to wait. There was a sudden commotion outside. Then in streamed my priestess, Melea, followed by another girl. I kissed Melea, and for good measure the other girl too. They were strikingly similar. Noticing the picture on the wall Melea said something in a strange language. She went to the keyboard on the wall and punched a few buttons. The picture disappeared. Something else must have happened, for there were a few small clicks, but I didn't notice anything by eye. Then Melea made quite a little speech, again in the strange language. A second or two after she had finished I was astonished to hear her voice again in the room. I say in the room because it didn't come from any particular place. I suppose there must have been a lot of small speakers distributed everywhere over the walls. The astonishing thing was that the language was English, with a very curious pronunciation, but English nevertheless.

'This is my friend Neria. She too was in Greece, at the temple of Delphi. That also was a temple of Apollo. It was she who made the prophecy about the war between Athens and Sparta. Will you not introduce your friend?'

I began to speak in my not very good Greek. She interrupted me:

'It will be much better if you speak in your own language.'

So I made the introduction. Immediately I had finished there came my own voice, I would have sworn it was mine, in a language of which I didn't know a single word. Naturally I was pretty dumbfounded. The girls stepped forward and kissed John, one after the other, which must have surprised him as much as the language business did me. Off his guard, he turned to me and said:

'Did they behave in Greece like this?' Immediately after he had finished, his voice was heard everywhere throughout the room in the new language. The girls made the incident into a joke which helped break the ice. I've noticed before that when you've been close and intimate with a girl you haven't known for more than a short time the second meeting is always a slight embarrassment. One can never be sure whether the situation is still the same as it had been. So I was glad this moment of embarrassment was out of the way.

Melea turned to me and smiled. 'We have brought you a present. In fact we've brought you two, one from each of us, but we are only going to let you see one at a time.'

The translation system made for very accurate understanding but I could see it was going to be a bit stilted. It wouldn't be right over breakfast.

Now it was Neria who went to the keyboard. With a

deliberate flourish of the hand she tapped away at two or three of the buttons. I was quite unprepared for what followed. I suppose I expected some kind of picture to appear on the wall. But no, in through the doorway from the direction of the kitchen an object glided into the room. It made no sound as it moved. Neria pressed a button and it stopped not far from the exit on to the balcony. I realized they must have the magnetic tracks John was talking about even under the damned floor itself.

We all turned our attention to the object. At the touch of a switch on its side the top folded back. There underneath was a keyboard, a piano keyboard, with the usual eighty-eight keys. At the right-hand end there was a small metal lever, and nothing else.

The two girls stood waiting like expectant children at a party, just after the conjurer had arrived. For me, some conjuring would be necessary it seemed. There was no piano stool, no pedals, and the box itself just wasn't big enough to contain any appreciable length of string.

'Where do I sit?'

'Haven't you got an adjuster?'

'No,' said John, before I could reply.

The girls laughed. 'Then he is going to be very uncomfortable unless we fetch one from the storage room.'

We all made quite a business of adjusting the shape of the floor to fit the position of the box. It was every bit as impressive as the usual adjustment of the piano stool. At last I decided I was comfortable enough and that my hands were in the right relation to the keyboard.

The three of them were sprawling on the floor, Melea actually at a height above me, so contoured was the room. I felt as if I was in a kind of arena. I began to play a Handel chaconne. The effect was indescribable, indescribably good and indescribably bad. Sometimes the music came through with a really wonderful tone. Then an instant later there would be the most horrible overload effect, the volume would become enormous. I stopped for a moment.

'You'd better either adjust the control or play more lightly,' said Neria.

I tried moving the lever. As I did so, the pressure needed on the keys to give the same volume of tone changed. I began to experiment with single notes. It was the pressure on the key that decided the volume. Any increase of pressure after a key reached its bed, any key-bedding, produced a grotesque increase of output. The mechanics of striking a single note were completely different from a piano. On the piano you get maximum output at the moment the hammer hits the strings. From that moment on, the volume of tone sags badly. A long-sustained note is impossible if you judge by an objective criterion. The thing which makes piano music possible is the curious subjective effect by which you continue to think you hear the tone after it has really sagged. Of course the manner of striking the strings makes some difference but the appalling fall-off of tonal quality is always there. Here the situation was quite different. The volume could be held steady, for seconds if necessary, simply by keeping a constant downward pressure on the key. In fact by increasing the pressure you could increase the output, exactly as a violinist can.

It took a lot of experimenting before I had the feel of it. Indeed it would be weeks or months before I would be able to get maximum effects out of this new system. In a sense it was a little like switching from piano to organ, in that the sound stopped as soon as you took your finger off the key. Unlike the organ, however, you could get a surge of tone in the middle of a note, like the thrill a violinist can produce.

When I had got the hang of individual notes I found the general tonal structure had interesting differences and interesting possibilities. It was sharper, less vague than a piano. This seemed to come from control over high harmonics particularly in the treble. The general effect was a greater clarity and a more legato quality. The harsh percussive effects of the piano could not be reproduced, they were quite lost. I found by adjusting the general output control that I could either play with the usual kind of heavy pressure, the strong finger effect I was normally used to, or I could go over to quite light fingering as one does on a harpsichord. Either way I could get the same big volume of tone. This made it possible, using light fingering, to play passages both very fast and very loud.

I had to be almost literally pulled away from this new box of tricks. Apparently a meal was ready. Incredibly it was set on the floor. The girls had made all kinds of indentations to hold the various articles and dishes. The colours of the food stood out sharply against the dark blue flooring material. It looked exactly as if a bed of flowers had been laid out. The effect was so remarkable that I felt it could not be due to chance.

It was all entirely vegetarian food. They didn't eat animals John had said. Yet you wouldn't have known it. The tastes were there. In fact my only problem was there seemed to be too many tastes, almost as if you were getting the whole of a large menu all at once. The wine was very good. Apparently a span of ten thousand years made little difference so far as wine was concerned.

'How do you like your little present? You haven't thanked us for it yet.'

'He is exactly like a child with it,' said John with a tinge of jealousy.

I pressed my advantage. 'You said you had two presents.'

'None for me,' muttered John. At this the girl Neria stroked his face.

'There are better presents for you than a little black box,' Neria smiled.

I saw John was going to have his troubles, and especially because of the way the translation system operated. It suddenly struck me how much the pronunciation of English by the girls had changed. It was now very much more like normal everyday English. My curiosity flowed over and I had to ask how it was all done, although I realized we were pretending that nothing seemed unusual to us.

'Oh, it is really very simple,' said Melea.

'I would not have thought you would have had any difficulty with that,' grinned the other girl.

John took up the challenge. 'Let me make a guess. First you have a system of language translation set up in a computer. As well as grammatical rules, synonyms, and so forth, you have a library of mouth sounds. When a word is spoken it is analysed for its sounds, taken to pieces. Then it is put through the translation procedure. The same is done for the translated word, in reverse. It's a matter really of having sounds as well as a dictionary. But how did you manage to change the pronunciation as you went along?'

The same thing was puzzling me.

The girls laughed: 'Your own pronunciation was analysed, of course. As you spoke each word, the sound formation was taken to pieces. After that, when the same word was used in the translation of something that we said, it was put together in the way you had used. Now do you understand?'

John nodded, and I think I got a pretty good idea myself.

But there was still one thing that worried me. 'How do you get the voices to sound so right?'

'Because each of us has a library in our computer of the way our voice sounds. Not just in our own language, but of all the sounds that can be made with the human voice. By doing this our voice could be translated into any language whatever, even though we ourselves could not understand a word of it.'

'You haven't a library of our voices?'

'No, we are not really using your voices at all. We've used the voice of one of our own people, not anybody we happen to know well personally. Otherwise it would be very strange.'

By now we had finished the meal. I was again astonished by the speed with which it was all cleared away. Just the same carpet-sweeping procedure that John had used. The really striking thing was when the white strip reached the position of the piano, or rather the piano-like box of tricks, the whole thing lifted up off the floor, and the white strip went underneath it. Thirty seconds and the room was clear. Dinner was finished.

Both girls went out. Several minutes later they came back carrying two large parcels which they put on top of the piano. With smiles they bowed at me and said: 'They're yours.'

They were the most normal articles I had yet seen, apparently straightforward parcels, wrapped in what looked uncommonly like paper. I undid the first one. It was just a large metal disc about two feet in diameter and an inch thick.

'Handle it very carefully, please.'

John came over: 'It must be hollow, or layers of metal. Otherwise it would be much heavier.'

It had seemed heavy enough to me. I undid the other parcel. Here there were three discs of the same diameter but less thick. The girls were watching us with amusement. John and I talked about it for some time. It was obviously connected with some sort of electronic device. But what? They were like huge, weighty gramophone records, the sort of thing a stone-age man might have produced, only they were made of bright metal not stone. We gave it up.

Melea took the biggest of the discs, while her friend went to the keyboard on the wall. I was beginning to wonder what these people would do without their walls and floors, when a metallic arm moved smoothly and slowly out of the wall. Melea fitted the disc into it and the whole thing retreated completely from view.

There was a lot to be said for not cluttering up the room with chairs and tables and a hundred and one other articles. The room might have been expected to look bare but it didn't. This was due to the shape and the colours which somehow conveyed the impression of being out-of-doors. I realized what it was that had struck me as being so queer in the first place. Normally when you go into a building you change your sense of scale. Rooms that would seem ridiculously small if they were out-of-doors become tolerably large. What happened here was that you didn't make any change of scale, you had the same sense of size as you have in the open air.

I just had time for these reflections before the music started. I was transfixed at the first chords. It was the beginning of the Mass I had taken three months of the winter to write. It was all there, the whole orchestra. At least it was very nearly the orchestra as I knew it. Very nearly, but not quite, the harmonic balance of the individual instruments was a little different. The music flowed on and I lost all sense of calm judgement. Listening to one's own music is a little like listening to one's own voice, you do it with a sense of wonder, fascination, and horror. You can't believe it really sounds like that. The wonder now was that the instruments were all there, the notes all correct. I could detect no mistake of pitch or of timing. Indeed the timing was if anything too accurate. When the chorus came in the words were English. They were my own words.

Now we were at the section I had played in the temple, the section I had conceived of in an agony of mind. It held me now, playing on my emotions as if I, its creator, were no more than a keyboard. The pain and tragedy dissolved at last into sunlight and the work came to an end, after what seemed like a vast span of time. It was I suppose about two hours.

I knew of course what was on the other discs, the symphony and the piano pieces. I had no thought to hear them now, I wanted no more music that day. I took hold of Melea and we went out on to the balcony. There were no lights anywhere on the ground but the sky was incredibly full of stars. It was even clearer, more remote, than the Grecian sky had been.

It was like the night we had passed at the temple, last night so far as my memory was concerned. Even so there were a thousand and one questions I wanted to ask which still perturbed me, but this was not the occasion for them. The morning would come soon enough.

I woke first. Melea was still there, her face close to mine, her long hair entangling her shoulders. I lay without moving for some time, not wishing to waken her. The feeling was in part selfish for I wanted to study her face. There was natural beauty in it but not a trace of glamour. It was a face that could not have existed in the year 1966.

The eyes opened at last. There was the usual fleeting fraction of a second while the eyes come into focus and the brain comes to life.

'Today will be a happy day,' she said, a little sleepily. There was an emphasis on the word today which I could not understand.

It was indeed a good day. We started early, not long after sunrise. It turned out there was some reasonably shaped clothing in the house, a kind of shirt and trousers. Fashions can't change too much simply because of the shape of the human body. The odd thing about these clothes, however, was they had no buttons or fastenings of any kind. You put them on after the style of a boiler suit, except they were very well cut and there was no zip-fastener. There was a special kind of cloth along the fastening which simply pressed against the cloth on the other side of the seam. It was like scotch-tape, except you could use it time and time again. You simply pulled it apart with a good stout tug.

After the usual frothy breakfast we called up a taxi. Unlike the taxis I was used to, it wouldn't come to the house itself, only to the nearest taxi rank, a good mile away. There had been a heavy dew during the night which was still covering the trees, bushes, and flower beds as we walked down the hillside. The vehicle was already waiting for us. I can best describe it as a squashed sphere. The lower third of it was opaque, the rest was made of some translucent material. There was a little kiosk near by. Melea beckoned me to follow her. I watched

153

while she tapped out what I took to be our destination on one of the inevitable keyboards. A slip of material, translucent, about six inches long by one inch wide appeared. Set within the material were about a dozen characters, apparently in metal. We got into the vehicle. Melea pulled out a rectangular sheet about two feet long. Into this she inserted the smaller slip and then replaced the sheet. Neria touched a button and instantly we began to move.

I could see now as we moved away the reason for the squashed appearance of the sphere. The vehicle itself was about fifteen feet across. The walls were rather like the kind of shop window that doesn't seem to have any glass in it. You had the impression you were looking straight out. There was no rattle or rumble as we picked up speed. Very soon we were whistling along at what I guessed to be about eighty miles an hour. It took about two hours to our destination. We went towards the south. I could see the big mountains I had glimpsed from the balcony. They were volcanic cones, not unlike the mountains of Hawaii in fact.

'One of them will be Popocatepetl, I suppose,' said John.

'They must have cleared the whole of the jungle that used to occupy these parts,' he added.

We passed mainly through green fields. Every now and then I could see little valleys filled with flowers, like the one we had come from. I thought I could glimpse houses. Also in the distance I caught flashes of vehicles similar to the one we were travelling in. At an intersection of the pathways, or magnetic tracks, or whatever they were, we came quite close to another vehicle. The occupants waved and we waved back.

As we approached the mountains it was obvious the jungle had indeed been cleared. We went quite smoothly and silently up the mountainside. Eventually we passed from fields to grassland. It was for all the world like an alp, except there were no animals.

'What has happened to all the animals?'

I asked this in Greek, for Greek was now our only means of communication – strange we had to work through a language that lay two thousand years in the past for me, eight thousand years in the past for the girls.

'The situation is very sad. All the major animals were wiped out and became extinct long ago.'

'How about the domestic animals?'

'We no longer have any need of them. They are not here, not in our country anyway. We turned them loose in places suited to them. Many exist in a wild form like cattle and sheep, but the animal population of the Earth has become very poor. At least it was so until these new events occurred. Now we have collected them again.'

We reached our destination high on the grasslands. I could feel the altitude quite appreciably, which meant we were probably above eleven thousand feet. Grass still grew at this elevation because of the sub-tropical climate. For about three hours we climbed along a pleasant track. At last we came to rougher ground. There was a hut where we had lunch. We took exactly what we needed. I was now keenly aware that nobody ever paid for anything.

When I remarked on this to John he said, 'Obviously this is a high-powered civilization with very few people. I imagine they could make far more than they need, so why worry about paying.'

'To make sure people work.'

'It's obvious they have so many machines, so much automation, there isn't any need for anybody to work, not in our sense. I imagine their problem must be leisure not work.'

Another party arrived, a party of six. They looked at us curiously and I thought a little sadly. I couldn't make out why for I didn't feel sad myself. The newcomers had a remarkable family resemblance to the two girls. These people must all look pretty much alike. The man who had appeared for a brief moment back in the temple on the mountain, he also had been remarkably like Melea. I saw now why the girls didn't bother to glamorize themselves. If everybody looked more or less the same, there really wouldn't be any point in it.

I asked Melea how many people there were in total. She told me about five million.

'Over the whole Earth, only five million?' I asked in astonishment.

'We don't live over the whole Earth, only in this country here.'

'You mean the rest of the Earth is empty?'

'Not empty but wild, in its natural state. Why should we want to live everywhere? Five millions is quite enough people to know. How many people do you know in your country, more than five million?'

'Of course not. We make a choice of those we wish to know.'

'There is no point in us making such a choice. Why should we want to know one person and ignore another?'

The view away to the north was tremendous as we walked back again downhill by a different path.

'I think we must hurry,' said Neria.

This was translated to us, with the explanation that there would be a thunderstorm about four o'clock in the afternoon. We got back to our taxi barely in time. It was a wonderful ride down the mountainside through the driving rain and the flickering lightning. Several times the lightning struck at points not far removed from us. Neither of the girls seemed at all worried about being hit ourselves. John noticed this and whispered, 'They must have some protective field, lowering the potential a bit, near the track.'

It was amazing there was so little noise inside our sphere.

Once we quitted the vehicle back at our own valley we soon got thoroughly wet. The girls didn't seem to mind in the least and strode along, uncaring. We followed them to a house which wasn't ours. Quite a few people were already here. One of them showed us to what seemed to be a changing-room. There was a strong hot-air blower that dried you off completely in a couple of minutes. Then we picked ourselves a selection of garments and sealed ourselves up inside them. We took less than ten minutes but it could have been done in under three or four.

About twenty people came in that evening to what was evidently a party. It was not quite as free and easy as a party can be where everybody speaks the same language, because quite often we had to go through the translation system. Yet it was all far, far easier than attending any sort of function in a foreign country in the world of 1966. I had been right about the preparation of meals. They all made a big thing about the arrangement of the colours, into patterns like flower beds, and about the shape of the floor. They divided into two halves and had a kind of race. From the gun it took about ten minutes.

During the meal a sly game went on, of softening up the floor under one or another of us. It may sound ridiculous but it certainly looked funny, especially after a modicum of alcohol. Although everybody talked twenty to the dozen there was no appalling volume of sound. The floor, the ceiling, and the walls, were evidently sound absorbing. Yet when I had played the previous night I hadn't had the impression of playing into a sink. It seemed as if the reflecting qualities of the room must be changeable.

After dinner the little piano suddenly appeared. It came in by itself through a doorway. There was nothing for it but that I should sing for my supper. There was a very good reason why everybody wanted to hear me. What I had already begun to suspect, that nobody in this society played any musical instrument, was confirmed. Music could be put together so readily using electronic techniques that incentive was quite lacking for anyone to go through the long years of drudgery so necessary for proficient performance.

The evening reminded me in a curiously vivid way of the party back so long ago in Los Angeles. I found myself beginning the waltz theme of the Diabelli variations. I had not played them since the night in Los Angeles. Until now I had associated Beethoven's great masterpiece with a different time, a different age. But now the variations emerged with as much freshness as ever, and with more power than I had been able to produce on the instruments of that apparently far-off epoch.

14   Grave e Mesto

The following morning the party had quite dissolved. When Melea and I appeared for breakfast we found John talking to a white-haired man of about sixty. Melea instantly became serious. She said:

'This morning it has to be different. It is about the film we stopped you from seeing the other afternoon. You will soon understand why it was better left until the end.'

This made me uneasy.

'What do you mean, by there being an end?'

'I think you must see first. After that you must hear what we have to say. Then we can decide.'

The two girls and the man left us. The beginning of the film appeared. Evidently the others didn't want to watch it.

The showing took upward of four hours. It was the longest documentary film I had ever seen, naturally enough for it dealt with a time span of six thousand years. We covered time at an average rate of a century to each four minutes. There was no place here for intricate involvements, or for the niceties of politics. Yet it was all too easy to follow. The black record of the human species swept remorselessly on as the minutes and hours ticked away.

It was a shock at the beginning to be very quickly out of both the twentieth and the twenty-first centuries. The first quick point was a transition from poverty to affluence in the undeveloped continents of the twentieth century, Africa and Asia. A homogeneous civilization swept with incredible speed over the whole Earth. There were brief flashes of the people, of their machines, their customs, their political leaders. It was all done visually. We sat in silence watching, our ears free of the cacophonous uproar of the usual sound track. It was easy to comment to each other on what we saw, not that we had much to say beyond the occasional exclamation.

Earth teemed with people. Cities spread out farther and

farther until they became joined to each other. Urban populations covered an increasing fraction of the land surface. At first it was only one per cent, then five per cent, then twenty-five per cent. The technological drive went irresistibly on. Land became of more and more value. There was no room any longer for any animal save man. So we watched the gradual extinction of the whole animal world. Even the bird population declined and withered away.

We saw something of domestic life. We saw the standardized little boxes in which almost everybody was now living. The insistent question formed in your mind, what was it all good for? What conceivable reason could there be to prefer a thousand little boxes to one dignified house? The same of course for the people. What was the advantage of this appalling fecundity of the human species?

Soon we were in the twenty-fifth century. Angry voices began to be heard. The pressures were mounting, competing with the technology. The technology itself was kept going by the most rigorous demands on individual freedom. It was indeed a veritable ant-heap. The average person became restricted to a life that lay somewhere between the freedom of the twentieth century and the lack of freedom of a man serving a life sentence in prison. Nobody travelled now, except on official business – I mean travelled to distant parts. Everything was provided in one's own locality, food, amusements, work. The work itself demanded little initiative. The people were leading what can only be described as a punched-card life.

The technology wasn't working too well any more. Food was mostly of poor quality, mostly factory produced. At that stage, in the twenty-fifth century, the seas were essentially swept clean of fish. The land animals had been the first to go, then the birds, now last the fish.

The first disaster happened with amazing suddenness. What had seemed a more or less homogeneous civilization split into two, like the division of an amoeba.

'It's a point of instability,' whispered John. 'Look, the whole thing's going to grow exponentially.'

Whatever he meant, this vast gargantuan, sprawling, tasteless, in every way appalling, civilization exploded in a flash. It started with bombs and rockets, with fire. The film, so far silent, now came alive, not with any synthetic sound track, but with the crackling of the actual fire, with the shriek, instantly cut short, of a woman enveloped in a cloud of burning petrol. Then it was all over. It was quiet everywhere. Death and decay swept at an incredible speed, like some monstrous fungus, everywhere over the Earth. There was no movement, no transport, no food distribution. The intricate organization which had itself fed on the efforts of a large fraction of the whole population was dead. Everything which had depended on it, including the lives of the people, now died too. We could hear the whine of infants, the despairing cries of children. The abomination came at last to an end. It seemed as if the human species, having wiped everything else from the face of the planet, had now itself become extinct.

Miraculously this did not happen. A dozen or more specially favoured, especially lucky, small centres of population managed to survive. They were already beginning their recovery by the time we saw them, I suppose because no camera had been there to record the worst moments. Indeed the technique of photography suddenly became very crude, almost the way it had been when photography was first invented.

We saw the slow steady expansion of one centre after another. The population increased, the technology improved. We saw the people happy and smiling again. We heard them talking in a new language. We saw them attempting to recover the relics and treasures of the past, particularly books and manuscripts. We saw how they made every effort as they improved to absorb the culture of the past. Amazingly, a great deal survived.

By now we were almost a thousand years on. The new civilization was becoming exuberant. There was nothing of the deathly, machine-like quality of the situation before the first upheaval, the Great Disaster as it came to be known. People were individuals again. There was hope for the future once more.

The different centres were by now overlapping each other. They were in argument. There was a period of war, astonishingly short it seemed to us on this kaleidoscopic record. The war turned out to be no more than a kind of lubricant that allowed the hitherto separate regions to join up with each other into a coherent whole. With a growing sense of horror I realized it was all going to happen again. There was going to be a second disaster. It became so completely inevitable as one watched. Century after century went by. Each brought its contribution to the elephantine growth. Gone was the zip and zest of the first pioneers of this new civilization. We were back again in a punched-card era. It all happened with horrible predictability. The first and second catastrophes might have been interchanged and you couldn't have told the difference.

So it was with the reconstruction. We saw it all beginning again. There was a longish sequence belonging to North America, in what used to be the United States. It had a vaguely familiar look about it. John burst out loudly, in contrast to our previous whispers:

'That's it, look, that's it! That's what we saw, when we flew across America from Hawaii!'

So it was. What we had seen was not the America of the eighteenth century. It was the America of the fourth millennium.

The record was relentless. I could see now why the girls and the white-haired man had not wanted to stay. Added to horror of intimate detail, I had the feeling of a whole species in some monstrous, unclean cycle from which it could never escape. Each cycle was occupying a little less than a thousand years. Always during the reconstruction phase we could see the same bland confidence that this time it would be different. Because these phases were reasonably long drawn out, over three centuries or so, it always seemed as if the disease had been cured. Then quite suddenly, almost in a flash, the monstrous expansion started again. It was a kind of shocking social cancer. Then came the major surgery of flame and death, and so back to endeavour, to a temporary happiness, and to unrequited hope.

Yet at last something different did happen. At last, when it seemed as if extinction had finally come, just two centres managed to survive. They grew to a reasonable and moderate size, and at that they stopped, or almost stopped, for nearly a thousand years. The film became quite detailed. An important point had evidently been reached.

Always when a centre of population expanded from a small beginning the people were far less heterogeneous than the kind of human population we were used to. Now we had a rather uniform situation. Yet there were still the two population centres.

There was no suggestion of war, however. The people, looking much like the people of the future, were restrained and reasonable, they had learnt the lesson of the past. The two centres maintained a quite friendly rivalry, with the aspects of a favourable situation about it. The rivalry seemed to prevent complacency, it seemed to provide an incentive to achievement. Yet as time went by I could detect a slow steady growth in both population groups, caused apparently by the friendly competition between them.

Both groups were quite well aware of what was happening. They noted the growth, yet they decided after considerable thought that the situation could be kept within bounds. So it was for a long time. Quite suddenly, however, control seemed to be lost. There was a stage beyond which expansion simply could not be prevented. This stage was reached before anybody expected it. From then on we watched a wretched society being forced along a road down which it did not wish to travel. It seemed as if everybody knew what was going to happen, yet nobody could prevent it.

'They've got beyond a point of instability. It's inherent in the organization. They can't get back.'

John's prognostication was right. The controlled rivalry disappeared. In its place came an unrestrained rivalry. The groups grew, merged together, after the usual momentary outburst, and so the disease spread to its inevitable conclusion.

At the next re-expansion phase there were three groups. When they reached a very moderate size, about a million people each, discussions took place between them. The outcome was that all three groups merged voluntarily, not to cover the whole Earth, but to contain themselves in a small portion of it. So the people of the future at last appeared. I saw clearly now why they lived in only one place.

How long had they been in their present state? It turned out, upward of a thousand years. In that time strikingly little change had taken place. They believed a genuine stability had at last been achieved, and their belief had more substance to it than the facile, arrogant claims we had seen so often in the earlier parts of the film.

We sat for a long time in silence. There did not seem very

much to say. Maybe an hour later, the girls and the white-haired man returned.

'I think the time has come for us to speak seriously,' said the man.

I could see something of the appalling predicament that he and his people were in. It was clear the Earth, with its different centres of population, might already be beyond all control. John was evidently thinking along the same lines, for he asked:

'What plans have you made, about how you're going to organize the Earth?'

The white-haired man answered simply: 'We have no such plans, because none are possible.'

The horror of the situation was at last becoming clear to me. It wasn't so much that we, the remnants of the twentieth century world, were inevitably condemned to a catastrophic future, with its rhythmic disasters, but that these people, the people of the future, were condemned to return to the agony of the past.

I could see the hopelessness of trying to impose any kind of control. It might last for a few years, even for a few generations, but from what we had seen there could be no permanent stability. Sooner or later the same grotesque swings, from arrogant expansion to pitiful collapse, would occur. It could only be prevented through the gross annihilation of the whole of the past. I had no doubt the technology of these people would enable them to carry through such an annihilation. Yet this was just as impossible as any attempt at control. It would destroy, psychologically, the annihilators. It would be a complete negation of all that these people stood for.

John had been silent for a while, evidently in perturbed thought. Now he asked, surprisingly, 'Have you seen the situation in Africa and in the southern hemisphere?'

'Yes, we have made a survey.'

'What did you find?'

'Nothing, the same as you.'

'Isn't that a bit odd? I know you have elected to live here in this part of the world. But surely some of your people, if only small expeditions, must have explored other parts of the world fairly frequently?'

'You are wondering why neither you nor we have run into any of our expeditions. The point has not escaped us.'

'What's your explanation?'

'We know of nothing definite.'

John was pacing about restlessly. He was evidently much agitated. Dramatically he turned. 'You know what I think, I think both Africa and the southern hemisphere belong to the future, like the great Plain of Glass. I don't think they're your contemporary world at all. Otherwise there would be unmistakable traces of your people somewhere.'

The white-haired man smiled a little sadly.

'You are very intelligent, Dr Sinclair. There seems to be little that has escaped you. Yes, it is possible that those regions may represent the future, the future even to us.'

'You realize the implication?'

'Naturally.'

I could contain myself no longer. 'For heaven's sake what does it mean?'

John turned on me. 'It means that in the future, in the time belonging to those lands, the human race has become extinct. It has all come to nothing, the great experiment of animal life on this planet. Nothing has survived except a few insects.'

'I do not see why you should be so perturbed, Dr Sinclair.'

'It is a confession of failure.'

'I cannot see why. In that sense, failure must come in any case, quite inevitably. You yourself have stood on the great Plain of Glass. You know what the whole Earth will come to in the end. The only question is whether it comes later, or sooner.'

I turned incredulously. 'Extinction! It doesn't worry you?'

'In the sense of a serious critical problem, no. It will be hard for you to understand our point of view. In your time, everything of importance always lay in the future. You worked for the future, you were dominated by a sense of progress. The path along which you walked was always less important than the view around the next corner. Our philosophy is quite different. We have strong ideas of how life should be lived. If the conditions we believe to be necessary can no longer be met we would prefer there to be no future. You see, we do not believe in time as an ever-rolling stream. We believe all times are equally important, the past is not lost.'

I looked quizzically at John, for this was much what he himself had said one afternoon back in England. I remembered his argument about consciousness and about rows of pigeon holes, except I couldn't remember the details. Whether because he actually agreed with the white-haired man, or because he thought I had detected him in some inconsistency, John now took a different line.

'I could sympathize with your point of view if you could be sure extinction will come quickly. Do you think that will be the way of it? Surely there will be a long slow downward trend, at any rate to begin with. The degeneration will occur by slow creeping degrees. Things will go just a little wrong at first, then more wrong, then catastrophically wrong. We have seen enough today to be sure our species will not die easily. Extinction will be a long-drawn-out, agonizing affair. Surely you can't maintain that living through such an experience would be in any way pleasant? Surely it is to be avoided, if it possibly can be?'

The white-haired man fell silent. I could see John's point had great force with him. The girl Neria took up the argument:

'These are exactly the questions we have been occupied with during the past months. We have only come to a decision after much discussion.'

The white-haired man continued. 'It is only fair to tell you that what we are now saying is being heard by all our people.'

He pointed to the walls of the room as if to signify their qualities as receiving and transmission systems, qualities that were really obvious from the translations we were receiving.

He went on, 'I tell you this to make it clear that I am not giving just a personal opinion. These are the considered views of our whole community.'

'So what it comes down to,' said John, 'is that you're not going to do anything definite. You're going to continue in the same way as before?'

'You are correct. We have weighed the likelihood of extinction against all the other factors. We see that a general mixing of ourselves with the people of Europe might be said to give the human species another chance. But it would only be a blind chance.'

'It may be better to take even a blind chance.'

165

'With the certainty of a repetition of what you have just seen?'

We were back at the dilemma.

'Is there no way of proceeding slowly, of making experiments as you go?' I asked. For answer, the white-haired man went on:

'It is necessary for me to tell you something further, which I do not think you have yet appreciated. This strange world, this world with different ages living side by side, is not going to last permanently. Soon we shall revert to where we were before, or very nearly to where we were before.'

John nodded. 'Yes, I've been having suspicions in that direction. The question is, whose world is it going to be?'

'There can be no doubt at all about that. It will be ours. The play is already complete so far as you are concerned. There is no possibility of changing your society. It is we who are balanced on the knife edge.'

Deep within me I had the concept of there being some sort of plan.

When I said so, the white-haired man answered, 'The concept of a plan involves the idea of working to a specified end. You have in mind an ultimate El Dorado, which some day you may attain. Yet there can be no such El Dorado for the Earth. You have seen the final state of the Earth, out there in the great Plain of Glass. Perhaps you may think we could escape to some other planet moving around some other star. Yet that star too will die. So it will be for our whole galaxy. Ultimate continuity, in a physical, material respect is impossible.

'It is possible that gradually, inevitably, a huge intellect is being built from the creatures evolving on trillions of planets, everywhere throughout the universe. What in these circumstances you wonder would be our personal contribution? Perhaps if we were lucky we might contribute some small fragment to the sum total. More likely, we should contribute nothing. In all respects duplication occurs on an enormous scale, galaxies, stars, planets, living creatures, all in vast numbers. Stars like each other, living creatures like each other, all doing more or less the same thing, many indeed following almost exactly the same course of evolution. Yet, like the occasional mutation, something a little different may happen in exceptional cases. Perhaps in one case in a thousand a new facet may emerge. The question we have asked ourselves is whether this small chance is worth all the agony. Is it worth even the few thousand years you have observed this morning? Was the long process of evolution, lasting hundreds of millions of years, perhaps still to go on for hundreds of millions of years, worth the eventual small chance of life here on the Earth making a fragmentary contribution to some higher level of attainment, of which we can barely conceive? To an imaginary planner, the answer would of course be yes, because the planner would be interested only in the higher levels being built from the lower, just as we ourselves are pleased to have evolved from more primitive creatures. Yet to the creatures themselves the answer may be no.'

I saw now where the argument was leading. 'Your answer I take it is no?'

'Our answer is no. If we hold firmly with the utmost determination to our present point of balance we may hope to deny what we believe to be the normal course of evolution.'

John was walking up and down. 'Can we come back now to the how and the why of it?'

'There are several interpretations. It could be an opportunity to repair some biological defect in our heredity. We may have lost some essential component which your population has still within it. It could be a punishment, by showing us our own extinction, to cause us distress. It could even be an experiment to see how we react in the face of both these things.'

'Surely we're faced now with a situation that doesn't concern you alone? Your technology is naturally better than ours, but there are now at least twenty times as many people in our world as there are in yours.'

'That is quite incorrect I am afraid. Your people exist only in a ghost world. For a little while your world may have a vivid reality, but very soon now, now that we have made our decision, it will be gone. It will go in a brief flash, just as it arrived.'

I found it difficult to conceive of myself as a ghost. 'I would not have said there was anything ghostlike about the two of us.'

'Not in the least, you are real enough.'

Melea spoke for the first time. 'The different zones of the Earth will change back to what they were before. The Greece in which we met, the temple, will be gone. It will be gone far more completely than even the ruined remains of your own time. It will be gone almost without trace. It will be gone, except for the records in our libraries. Europe too will be gone, so will the great Plain of Glass. It will only be this zone here that will remain.'

The man nodded and went on, 'So you must decide. For the people of your country there is no decision to make. For us, we have made our decision. But for you it will be difficult. If you leave here you will disappear, into oblivion. If you stay, you will continue to live out your lives among us. The decision you will take must depend on your own thoughts and emotions. We cannot guide you further. Between you there is both reason and emotion. You must find where *your* balance lies.'

Before they left, Melea came to me and said, 'I will not stay with you tonight, because I do not want to influence the way you will decide.'

The three of them, the two girls and the white-haired man, looking almost infinitely sad, left us to our thoughts and deliberations.

My first reaction was to question what had been said. 'Is there any possibility of it not turning out the way they think? I mean about Britain and Europe simply disappearing. It seems preposterous.'

'Well, it's only the inverse of what happened before. If it was possible to go one way, it must be possible to go the other.'

'But everything back home, John, it was real enough. Those weren't ghost people, they were people with real feelings.'

'Of course they had real feelings, but they were apparitions nevertheless. For us it's different. We shall live out a perfectly real life if we stay here, but only if we stay here.'

'Well, there can't be any doubt about it. Going back – to oblivion I mean.'

'That was the way I felt until I began to think about it. What you must realize is, you really wouldn't be going back to oblivion, you'd be going back to one life not two.'

'I don't understand, even faintly.'

'Surely you could see from the film we've just watched that we've already lived our proper lives. Our lives exist – you remember the pigeon hole business – lives in which we quitted

Los Angeles for Hawaii. Somewhere in Hawaii there was a forking point. Instead of a single set of pigeon holes, suddenly there became two sets. One of them went along perfectly normal lines.'

'You mean the lines we expected, a life in which we returned to the Los Angeles of the twentieth century?'

'Yes, of course.'

'Why don't we know anything about it?'

'Because the two have separated, they've forked apart. There's no connexion between them. You're either in the one or the other. It's the sequence all over again. Whichever you're in you never know of the other. In this sequence you can never know what happened when you returned to Los Angeles. In that other sequence you can never know even a single thing about this one. The two are utterly separated. In the other sequence, neither you nor I will know about the future, about the film we saw this morning.'

'Then what does it come down to? What's the decision?'

'The decision is whether we want this particular sequence to end in a kind of cul-de-sac. We can either prolong it out into the usual lifetime or we can simply chop it off.'

'What would be the sense of chopping it off?'

'Because we might find this sequence intensely painful. Let me put it to you this way. You know you've got two lives to live. One life is perfectly normal and pleasant, but in the other you commit some serious offence, an offence which carries either the death penalty or a penalty of life imprisonment. You have the choice of which it shall be. If you only had one single life you might well choose imprisonment, in order to be able to go on. But with two lives do you really make that choice? There would be a lot to be said for avoiding the continual agony of being cooped up in prison, without any possibility of escape, year after year for several decades. You might well say to yourself – remembering you know about the other more or less pleasant life – let's make an end of this one, let's make it into a cul-de-sac. You see my point?'

'Except I don't see any parallel between being in prison and being here.'

'That's exactly the thing we've got to decide. That's exactly what our friend meant by saying we've got a difficult decision. I'm going to argue in favour of us both leaving. You take the other line. Then we must sleep on it and each make up his own mind about it.'

So we started. It was a long talk, very long, so I will give only a condensed version of what John said.

'Try to see what we're in,' began John. 'We're in a fossilized society. They've decided, completely as a matter of policy, that they're not going to change. They're not going to seek after progress. They're satisfied with the way life is. For them this may be fine but to us it would be a living death. We have a drive that forces us towards further achievement. Of course it may be quite illusory, probably it is. But being the way we are I think we would find it very much an imprisonment.'

'I don't see there's anything to stop us from going on doing the things we want to do.'

'I see plenty. I've got several thousand years of scientific development to learn before I could possibly get down to any really useful work. Of course it would be interesting enough to begin with. There'd be the solution to the problems that I know about. In a way it would be marvellous to read about it all. But just think of the years of grind and drudgery that would be needed before I could do anything at all creative. It's likely I'd never succeed. You've got to begin as a child, with a child's ability to learn, if you're to break through the wall of an entirely new civilization. I'm afraid I should be reduced to a useless potterer.

'You yourself may be a little better off. The kind of music you know of has some validity. In fact you've got more or less a completely open field. Yet even your position wouldn't be too good. These people may have a liking for music, they may be able to compose it, but none of them can actually play. You can see for yourself that everything is done electronically. Perhaps you would get them to sing but that would be about all. You would never hear a real orchestra again.

'These are the bigger issues but think of the smaller ones. There are a million and one simple things these people take for granted. Yet they'd all be strange to us. It's fine enough for a few days, but think how it'd be for a whole lifetime. We'd never really belong. We'd never again hear our own language spoken, except through an artificial electronic device. Remember Art Clementi and his boys. Remember the night you were first in La Jolla. It was all very wild and woolly maybe compared to these people. But wouldn't you come to ache for some of the zip and zest of that old life? In a way it was very squalid, but it had a vigour we should miss terribly. Remember we're not just walking out into nothingness. We're simply saying that this is a life we don't want to live, just as these people themselves have refused to follow a life of what we are pleased to call progress. Logically I can go along with them, but emotionally I'm not conditioned to their sort of existence.'

This is the main substance of what he said. I lay awake a long time that night. Even when I did get to sleep it was a troubled sleep. It was clear to me that John had already made up his mind to leave. If I stayed I'd be entirely alone. The point about never again hearing my own language hit me heavily, more than some of the logical arguments. It was true that within a few months or a year I would learn the language of these people, just as I had learnt to get along in Greek. But obviously there would always be a hankering back to the language of my youth.

I saw I would make pilgrimages back to my old home. There would be nothing but wild country. The glens of the Highlands would be much the same as I had known them. The shape of the hills would be the same. There would still be the hidden valley down which John and I had walked, apparently only a few months ago. But there would be no people, anywhere. I would make one or two such pilgrimages. Then I would go no longer, for the sadness of it all, the knowledge of what had happened, would be borne in on me too heavily. If I stayed here I would be in a kind of psychological no man's land. On the one side there would be a civilization which I liked but which I was not really a part of, on the other side there would be the vivid memories of my own people, and the knowledge of what they had come to suffer.

The following morning Melea and her friend were there. John told them we had decided to leave. Melea said that transportation arrangements had already been made. It was a sad little breakfast we had together. The time for departure came. We all agreed that delay would be bad. I took one last look around. There was the electronic box, the thing I had come to think of as a piano, looking now strangely pathetic. I had a strong urge to play on it for one last time. I told the others, saying I would prefer to be alone, that I would follow in a few minutes. Melea answered:

'Don't be too long. There isn't much time.'

I began to play. I realized that only in music could I find the answer I was seeking to the questions of the previous evening. Argument I could follow, it weighed with me, yet I could decide nothing from it. I did not know exactly what the music was, it was an improvisation not so much on a musical theme as on the agony of the destiny of man. I continued to play on and on, aware at last that I had made my commitment. I was playing the Schubert Andantino when Melea returned.

15 Coda

The prognostications were correct. Within a few hours of the departure of John Sinclair the world reverted to 'normal'. The England of 1966, the Europe of 1917, the Greece of 425 B.C., all vanished just as remarkably as they had appeared. I have not seen John again, nor do I think there is the smallest possibility I will ever do so.

Although much more science is known here than was known in the world of 1966, the detailed operation of the singular mixing of epochs is not well understood. As I make it out, issues involving time-reversal were involved, but the physics of the matter is not within my competence. What *is* quite certain is that the affair was brought about from a higher level of perception than our own. That such levels exist seems reasonable. That we ourselves are unable to comprehend the thoughts, the actions, the technology perhaps, of an intelligence of a higher order also seems reasonable. Disturb a stone and watch ants scurrying hither and thither underneath it. Can those ants comprehend what it is that has suddenly turned their tight little world upside down? I think not. It emerges very clearly that humanity can also be stirred up at any time, just like ants under a stone.

Two years have passed since these events. I have learned the new language. I no longer speak any English. For the most part this causes no distress. Yet occasionally a pang sears through me, an overriding desire to hear the old sounds again. I began this present narrative while in such a mood, feeling that if I couldn't speak my native language with any purpose I might at least write it.

In these two years I have composed a great deal of music. I do not compose nowadays for plaudits, for box office, or to please critics. I compose simply to please myself and my friends. I have returned to Europe, to England and even to Glencoe. I have climbed Bidean nam Bian again, followed the same ridge and come down into the same hidden valley. There is no village of Glencoe, no Macdonalds and Campbells to feud with each other, no motorists touring the glen. The country is entirely wild and still more beautiful.

More and more the old life has become vague and remote, like the memories of distant childhood. This gradual evaporation of a life which at one time was so intensely vibrant has come upon me with profound sadness. In these pages I have been able in some measure to give a sense of reality to what are now mere outlines in a gathering mist. Yet one detail stands out harsh and stark.

The day John Sinclair was missing from the caravan on the moors below Mickle Fell, I myself had the impression of a time gap of about two hours, between six and nine in the evening. I bitterly regret that I did not mention this impression to John. Of course I couldn't be at all sure I hadn't simply nodded off to sleep. I didn't want to appear to be dramatizing myself. Then subsequent events soon swept the incident out of my mind. Yet I suspect this small detail – reconsidered in the light of all that followed – assumes a deep significance. Accepting a bifurcation of worlds, accepting the copying process which John himself believed in so strongly, accepting his view that it was an apparition, a copy of himself, who returned to the caravan after the gap of nine hours, could it have been a copy of myself who was waiting there to receive him, another apparition who cooked the meal when he said he was so devilishly hungry?

After the bifurcation there were two worlds, the straight-forward world of 1966 in which nothing particularly unusual happened, and this strange new world belonging to the people of the future. Which of these worlds got our copies, which got the 'originals'? We both took it for granted that the copies went to the new world, copies of everything, of the Prime Minister, of our Australian pilot. This presumption may well have been correct except for the two of us. For us it may well have been the world of 1966 which had the apparitions.

Why the two of us? Why should just the two of us be different? Because we were just the two who managed to penetrate into the territory of the people of the future. John always thought of this penetration as accidental. He laughed about my getting through to Greece, about my encounter with

Melea in the temple on the hill. But was it really an accident? Hardly I think, for it fits too smoothly into a pattern, a pattern that would have been completed if John had elected to stay here, a pattern in which 'copies' vanished and 'originals' remained.

After the bifurcation in Hawaii, I was in the company of John Sinclair for a mere ten days. If at any time during those ten days I had looked for it I strongly suspect I would have found John's old birthmark. The birthmark was a tell-tale clue giving away the whole story. An opportunity did indeed fall our way, perhaps was even deliberately put in our way, the day of our trip to Popocatepetl, the day when we all got so very wet on the return journey. But for the sexual distraction of the two girls being there as we dried off, the mark would very probably have been noticed. I have no doubt now it was the real John Sinclair who was sent out from here – into oblivion. The irony and tragedy is that to the two of us it was the world of 1966 that was the real cul-de-sac.